D0009872

"Swear to me, Noah, that you'll never tell anybody that I was the guy who jumped into that truck and saved the Mercury house."

"But Donovan, people should know—"

"*Swear!*"

"All right, all right. I swear. I swear on the memory of Einstein, Max Planck, and Sir Isaac Newton."

And I had to be satisfied with that.

At home, I caught my first break of the entire morning. No one was up, and I was able to sneak back into my room unseen except by Beatrice. She lifted her fuzzy head from where she was sleeping next to Kandy and greeted me with a swish of her tail.

"The world almost ended today, kiddo," I told her, "but I think we got away with it."

Man, did I dream big.

# SUPERGIFTED

## GORDON KORMAN

BALZER + BRAY
*An Imprint of* HarperCollins*Publishers*

Balzer + Bray is an imprint of HarperCollins Publishers.

Supergifted
Copyright © 2018 by Gordon Korman
All rights reserved. Printed in the United States of America.
No part of this book may be used or reproduced in any manner whatsoever
without written permission except in the case of brief quotations embodied
in critical articles and reviews. For information address HarperCollins
Children's Books, a division of HarperCollins Publishers, 195 Broadway,
New York, NY 10007.
www.harpercollinschildrens.com

Library of Congress Control Number: 2017938673
ISBN 978-0-06-256386-6

Typography by Erin Fitzsimmons
19 20 21 22 23   PC/BRR   10 9 8 7 6 5 4 3 2 1
❖
First paperback edition, 2019

*For Amy Mendel,*
*Grand Dame of Gifted Education*

# 1

## SUPERGENIUS
### DONOVAN CURTIS

The problem with smart people is this: They can be really stupid 95 percent of the time.

To be fair, I'd only ever met one actual genius. But when that genius was Noah Youkilis, it counted as a full education on the subject.

A little background on Noah: He was the smartest kid by far in Hardcastle and possibly the whole world. We used to go to the Academy for Scholastic Distinction together—me by mistake and him because he actually belonged there. Actually, the Academy was way too easy for him. Even the gifted teachers agreed on that. When you had a 200-plus IQ, finding something to challenge you was the biggest challenge of all. For Noah, that challenge was getting himself kicked out of the Academy. And he succeeded with flying colors.

I wasn't smart enough to understand why Noah was so dead set on going to regular middle school, even though he explained it to me a bunch of times.

"Being a genius isn't hard," he told me earnestly. "What's hard is being normal."

He was 100 percent right about that. No one in the history of Hardcastle Middle School had ever been less "normal" than Noah Youkilis. He was short and skinny, with an eager, slightly bent posture that always reminded me of an oversize praying mantis. He was totally thrilled to be there, which instantly separated him from every other kid in the building. Plus he had a tendency to launch into a lecture at any time on any subject. Face it: He was a wedgie looking for a place to happen.

The craziest part was that the world's greatest genius wasn't doing so well in a school where the work was fifty times easier than his last one. He did all the math in his head, so he always lost points for not showing his work. He wrote his essay on *The Canterbury Tales* in Middle English and lost 78 percent for spelling errors. His programming skills were so advanced that none of the school's computers could handle his coding. In Hardcastle, most of the good equipment went to the Academy, not to this dump. All the teachers here knew about Noah was that nothing he did with technology ever worked.

"Noah, this is stupid!" I told him. "You're getting C's in a school where nobody's qualified to carry your pencil case!"

He was starry-eyed. "Isn't it great?"

"No, it's not great! It's not even good! At the Academy, you never sank as low as ninety-nine. Now you barely crack seventy."

"I'm average," he said blissfully.

"You're not even average for a genius," I shot back.

He looked wounded. "Do you know what it's like to be right *all* the time?"

"My brother-in-law lives with us," I informed him. "I'm not right *any* of the time." That was First Lieutenant Bradley Patterson, United States Marine Corps. More on him later.

"It's terrible," Noah said emotionally. "You know

the answers before anybody finishes asking the questions. You can't enjoy a movie because you can predict the ending during the opening credits. If it wasn't for YouTube there would be no surprise in my life ever."

"You're insane," I muttered.

His narrow praying-mantis shoulders hunched. "I knew you were going to say that."

"Well, you make it worse than it has to be," I accused. "You go out of your way to pick classes you're going to be bad at. Why did you have to sign up for wood shop?"

He drew himself up to his full four foot eleven. "I reject your theory that I'm bad at it. My salad bowl was a mathematical masterpiece—geometrically circular, with sides that rose to parabolic perfection."

"So how come you got a D?"

"There's nothing wrong with a D," he argued. "It's my first D. I love it."

"Daniel Sanderson said you hooked it onto the lathe wrong and it got launched through the wood shop window. By the time they tracked it down in the parking lot, it wasn't parabolic anything. It was toothpicks."

"It was what education is all about," he reasoned. "To you, a D means bad. To me, it means I have something to work toward."

"Like a bowl that's in one piece instead of nine hundred," I put in sourly.

"I've never had that before," he explained. "It's *empowering.* Just the thought that my work tomorrow, or next week, or next month might be *better* than my work today—that I can practice, and show improvement—it makes it worth getting out of bed in the morning."

I sort of understood, I guess. If you aced everything on the first try, you had nowhere to go but down. And Noah never even did that. He just stayed perfect. Until he landed in a school that didn't have a category for him.

I had to admit he was happy, though. Who was I to take that away from him?

So I assumed the next most important job—seeing to it that he didn't end up stuffed into a locker or hanging from a fence post by the waistband of his underwear. Hardcastle Middle School had a way of dealing with dweebs—all middle schools did, I guess. And a kid like Noah—the size of a fourth grader, the insect-like posture, the grating voice, the rocket-scientist vocabulary—had a real bull's-eye painted across his chest. Or he would have, if he'd had a chest.

To help me protect Noah, I enlisted my friends the

two Daniels—Daniel Sanderson and Daniel Nussbaum. They liked Noah—they thought he was entertaining, anyway. At least recruiting them as bodyguards reduced the number of potential bullies by two.

Three days a week, Noah and I rode the minibus to the Academy for Scholastic Distinction for robotics class. Believe it or not, the robotics team needed me almost as much as they needed Noah. Our latest robot, Heavy Metal, was operated via joystick, and I was the only team member who played enough video games to be good with a controller.

The usual crowd swarmed Heavy Metal. Chloe Garfinkle was oiling his Mecanum wheels, which had been squeaking. Jacey Halloran was adding fluid to the hydraulic system of his lifting arms. Noah and Abigail Lee were hunched over tethered laptops, pounding out the computer code of his operating system. Latrell Michaelson was polishing his stainless steel body with Windex. And then there was Oz—Mr. Osbourne, our robotics coach—making sure everybody in the lab was completely devoted to the care and well-being of Heavy Metal. We were the servants feeding him grapes and cooling his computer chips by waving palm fronds over him, like he was some ancient pharaoh.

It hit me—I was actually *jealous* of a robot! Sure, he was just a bucket of bolts and circuit boards, but he had the life. All he had to do was stand around while the smartest kids in the Academy agonized over how to make him better and stronger and faster than he already was.

My life? A little different.

For starters, my house, which was jam-packed these days. Brad, my sister's husband, was home between tours of duty in the Marine Corps. But since he was redeploying in a few months, there was no point in them getting their own place. So picture a smallish three-bedroom Cape with my parents; me; my sister, Katie Patterson; her six-foot-four husband; their baby, Tina, age two months; Brad's dog, Beatrice; and one more dog—Kandahar—all living in it. Kandahar was actually one of Beatrice's puppies. We had managed to unload all the others, but Brad had made us keep one. Now that he was a dad, he wanted to be a grandfather, too.

Get the picture? We had to walk sideways when we passed each other in the hall, and if we all got home at the same time, it practically took a shoehorn to get us in the front door.

Brad was a tank commander, a munitions specialist,

and a grand master at making my life miserable. He was an officer, used to barking orders and having people hop to it. Katie didn't mind. She was just thrilled to have him back. Mom and Dad were fine with it because he wasn't barking at them.

There were no newborn babies in the Marines, but that didn't stop Brad from trying to put Tina on the military schedule that he had up on our fridge:

*0600: Reveille*
*0605: Diaper change #1*
*0615: Morning feeding*
*0640: Burping*
*0645: Satisfactory burp produced*
*0700: Playtime—educational toys*
*0730: Initiate cleanup song*
*0815: Diaper change #2 (execute solid waste*
    *contingency, if necessary)*
*1015: Commence naptime sequence . . .*

Get the picture? Well, the very next day, Tina screamed for two solid hours, barfed all over her crib sheet, and blew through diaper changes one through six, all before reveille. At breakfast, Brad kept gazing longingly at the refrigerator door through bloodshot eyes with dark circles under them. He was looking at the schedule as if he couldn't believe it had let him down.

"You know, Brad," I commented, "Tina isn't in the military. Maybe General Patton raised his kid on a timetable like that, but Tina has other plans."

He glared at me. "When's the last time you had a haircut?"

Brad seemed to be obsessed with the last time I did a lot of things. The last time I did ten pushups. The last time I tucked my shirt in. The last time I used the word *sir*.

"When's the last time you gave somebody a break?" I shot back.

"I owe it to the men under my command to be hard on them," Brad lectured. "It could save their lives one day. The greatest gift you can give anyone is high expectations."

I had high expectations for him, too. I expected him to leave me alone. But nobody ever called it a gift. It was more like a pipe dream.

The worst part was that Mom, Dad, and Katie—my family—just sat there eating breakfast while Brad—who wasn't even really related—listed all my faults, one by one.

"So that's how it's going to be?" I asked. "Tina's too young to enlist in anything more military than Gymboree, so all Brad's commander instincts get switched to me?"

Katie yawned. Two hours' sleep did that to a new mother. "Come on, Donnie. Brad may be tough on you, but he does it out of love."

"Why can't Brad love somebody else for a change?" I mumbled.

Apparently, Brad had plenty of love to go around. He seemed to believe I was some kind of caterpillar, and enough hours or days or weeks or months of boot camp would transform me into a beautiful butterfly.

Brad had a military buzz cut and kept threatening to sneak into my room while I was sleeping and buzz me too. He exercised twenty-five hours a day and wanted me to do the same. Every morning when Tina woke him and Katie up at the crack of dawn, he would come into my room in his jogging shorts.

"Will I see you on the track this morning?"

In reply, I would mumble, "It's possible."

Just like, for example, whales might start doing sudoku and the moon might fall out of the sky, eradicating all life on earth. It was possible, but I wouldn't count on it.

Then Beatrice would growl him away—which was the one good thing about that dumb chow chow sleeping in my room. Despite the fact that Beatrice was Brad's dog, her list of grievances against him was almost as long as my own. First, he disappeared on her to go to Afghanistan. Then, when he finally came home, she wasn't even allowed in his room, since that was where baby Tina's crib was.

The fact that Beatrice liked me better than her actual owner was another item on the long list of things about me that got on Brad's nerves.

"Like it's my fault the hairball chose me to shed on after you and Brad kicked her out of your room," I complained to Katie.

"Of course it isn't." For once, my sister agreed with me. "We're grateful for all your help with Beatrice—and Kandy too. But deep down, Brad's heartbroken that he's lost the love he used to count on. And he can't help noticing who it's been transferred to." She looked at me pointedly.

"The dogs only love me because I let them take over my room. I'm their patsy more than anything else."

"Give me a break, Donnie. I haven't slept more than forty minutes at a stretch since we brought Tina home from the hospital."

I wasn't getting much sleep myself. When I inherited Beatrice, I got stuck with Kandy by default. You could ignore Beatrice, but Kandy was even younger than the baby. He was restless and hungry, and his new puppy teeth were just coming in, which made him whiny and irritable. His bowwow bone helped a little. It was a bright purple chew toy in the shape of a miniature dumbbell. I literally saw that thing in my sleep—it glowed in the dark. Worse, it squeaked—a piercing, high-pitched sound that felt like a piece of dental floss had been inserted in one of my ears and pulled out the other.

My theory: Kandy thought I was his mother. He was definitely dumb enough. And he needed a mom, because his own—Beatrice—wasn't very motherly. He followed me around like a bad smell. Whenever I sat still, he snuggled up next to me. Even my scent seemed to be a comfort to him. Never once did I enter my room without finding him trying to insert himself—drooling all the way—into one of my sneakers. Every night when I got into bed, he gazed at me imploringly. His big liquid eyes practically spoke: *Please let me up there with you!* He was so pathetic that I was almost tempted to give in. But let's face it, Kandy was about as toilet-trained as Tina. I wasn't *that* much of a sucker.

I tried to paper-train him. I spread out some newspapers, but all that taught him was how much he preferred peeing on carpet. The world was his toilet, and my room was his world.

He was named after the Afghan city where Brad was deployed. He was half chow chow, but we never met the dad. Great Dane maybe, or possibly Sasquatch. If he ever grew up around those giant paws, he was going to crowd the rest of us out of the house. Maybe he would mature into a majestic creature one day. For now, he was just plain funny-looking and so ungainly that all I heard half the night was *scramble-scramble-whump*, *scramble-scramble-whump* as he explored the room and his enormous feet kept tripping him up.

He had to be the homeliest, clumsiest, most infuriating mini-mutt on the face of the earth. I loved him, though. Only God knew why. Maybe because he kind of needed me. Katie and Brad were new parents and they had no time for him.

Besides, there was something in that *scramble-scramble-whump* that reminded me of myself. In those urgent, gung-ho steps you could tell Kandy thought he had it all figured out. Then—*whump*—he fell flat on his face. That was *me*. I was always getting in trouble for acting without considering the consequences. It was my fatal flaw.

The Daniels called it "fallout blindness."

That was my special connection to Kandy.

Tina had a lot more aunts and uncles than the average baby—unofficial ones, anyway. The entire Academy robotics team shared that honor. Katie had gone into labor in the middle of the state meet, and the team had ended up in the waiting room at the hospital while Tina was born.

Chloe and Noah visited the most often. Noah was obsessed with Tina the way he was obsessed with—in this order—YouTube, writing computer code, professional wrestling, and being average. Being obsessed was just what Noah did.

Noah was *different* when he was with Tina. He held her a little stiffly, like she was a prehistoric fossil that might turn to dust if handled too roughly. He didn't coo at her or talk baby talk. Instead, he recited scientific facts and formulas like "a floating object displaces its own weight in liquid," or "the square of the hypotenuse of a right-angled triangle is equal to the sum of the squares of the other two sides." For some reason, this brought out some of Tina's best toothless smiles.

"When she learns to talk, her first words are going to be 'E equals mc-two,'" predicted Sanderson.

"The two means *squared*, Einstein," Nussbaum corrected him.

The Daniels got a kick out of Noah. They got a kick out of everything. Some of the stuff I did had them rolling on the floor. Those two could make it through the end of the world so long as they had enough to laugh at.

With Noah around, they would never run short of material.

Lately, though, the Daniels had been getting annoyed with Noah. It was one thing to be entertained by him. It was quite another when he made them look bad in front of girls. Like when Noah accidentally flushed his glasses down the toilet. Sanderson had been using the stall next door. Noah told everyone who would listen how lucky he was that "my moment of crisis coincided with my friend Daniel's bowel movement." Or the time at lunch when he sneezed all over this girl Nussbaum was trying to sweet-talk, and then fumbled his asthma inhaler into her soup. While she scrambled to get herself cleaned up, Noah delivered a detailed scientific lecture on the strains of bacteria commonly found in human mucus.

"I like inhaler soup as much as the next guy," Nussbaum said angrily. "But not when it interferes with my love life."

"You don't have a love life," Noah pointed out helpfully.

Nussbaum was bitter. "Thanks to *you*."

For all his brains, Noah didn't pick up on their anger and impatience. He thought he was fitting in perfectly, and this was what regular school was like. Glasses down the toilet. Inhalers in the soup.

And that was how it was going—until the day the fire alarm went off.

The siren interrupted a social studies quiz, so it got a big cheer. We assumed it was a drill until we got out of the room to find the corridor filled with smoke. At that point, all our orderly filing turned into a mad scramble for the exit. My first whiff of the fumes nearly put me flat on the floor. It was rancid and spicy-sweet at the same time. What was on fire—the dumpster outside the cafeteria?

I was psyched. A nice unscheduled break from class and a little chaos besides. Chaos was kind of my specialty. It was usually pretty entertaining.

A flying figure came racing at me, knocking me into a bank of lockers. It was Sanderson, choking and gagging. Nussbaum was at his side, breathing into a paper towel.

"I quit!" Sanderson shouted over the clamor of the alarm. "It's a lost cause!"

"What's going on?" I demanded. "Where's the smoke coming from?"

"Like you don't know!" Nussbaum rasped.

"I *don't* know!"

At that moment, an unmistakable voice cried, "That's not just a soufflé—it's next generation data analysis!"

The Home and Careers room emptied out in a flash, Noah in the lead. His white apron was black with soot, and his face hadn't fared much better. His glasses were askew with one temple tangled in his hairnet as he ran down the hall, followed by an angry mob of classmates.

He slipped behind the three of us as his pursuers lost him in the smoke and thundered out the nearest exit.

It looked like the fun was ending already. "Jeez, Noah, what did you do?"

"Oh," said Noah, as if surprised at being asked, "my

program can sift through thousands of terabytes of information—"

Nussbaum was furious. "That's not terabytes I smell—it's sewer gas!"

"I devised an artificially intelligent program to scan every recipe on the internet to make a soufflé no one's ever made before."

"I wonder why!" Sanderson raged. "Because it explodes, maybe?"

"It didn't explode," said Noah with dignity. "It's just on fire. And," he added, dejected, "it fell."

Nussbaum faced me. "Sorry, Donovan, but you're on your own from now on. Yesterday somebody wrote 'loser' on my locker in Wite-Out. It means I'm getting blamed for *him*."

"That's totally unfair," Noah complained. "I have a C average."

Sanderson addressed Noah. "Sorry, kid. It's nothing personal. You were okay at the Academy for Scholastic Dorkstinction, but around here, you're a drag on our image. We can't help you anymore."

They headed out the door, bringing up the rear of Noah's cooking class.

Noah seemed bewildered. "What's that supposed to mean? I don't need help. I'm doing amazing. Do you realize how much room for improvement this leaves?"

A platoon of uniformed firefighters swarmed past us in the direction of the Home and Careers room.

I sighed. "I'll give you that, Noah. There's definitely room for improvement."

Noah glowed.

# 2
# SUPERSTOKED
## NOAH YOUKILIS

I used to go to the Academy for Scholastic Distinction, the top-rated gifted school in the state. According to Oz, my former homeroom teacher, I had the highest IQ any of the faculty had ever come across. They held weekly staff meetings on how to keep me stimulated and challenged. They even sent a group of teachers to a conference in Switzerland on how to motivate students at the highest rung of the intelligence ladder.

   I was bored out of my mind.

I once saw this video on YouTube where a kid was complaining about a classmate being a know-it-all, and I was amazed at how insensitive that was. It's no fun to be a know-it-all, because you *know it all*. You can never be surprised or shocked or scared or thrilled. Because whatever happens, you already saw it coming. Know-it-alls shouldn't annoy people; everybody should feel sorry for us and relieved they don't have this problem.

My teachers at the Academy threw the hardest stuff in the world at me, and I threw it right back at them. And none of it challenged me as much as one soufflé in Home and Careers at regular school.

My project was a triumph of data mining, distilling centuries of recipes into a list of ingredients no single chef could have come up with—things like cardamom and quail eggs, camel's milk and finely ground roasted durian seed. Scientifically, this should have been the most magnificent soufflé in the history of cooking. Instead, it burned like chlorine trifluoride, a key ingredient in rocket fuel. The fire chief commented that he hadn't smelled anything like that since the great fertilizer factory explosion of 2006.

My teacher, Mrs. Vezina, said, "You must be very disappointed, Noah."

How could I ever explain it to her? I wasn't disappointed; I was stoked! If I was bad at one thing, logic dictated that I could be bad at other things too. It was like discovering a whole new world.

There was an old song from the 1960s called "Be True to Your School" that always perplexed me. Why would anyone form a sentimental attachment to a building? There was nothing to be true to except bricks and mortar and glass and a few dozen other materials. But now I was starting to feel real affection for Hardcastle Middle School. It had to be the greatest school in the history of education. It was teaching me how to learn, when, before that, I didn't need to because I already knew it all.

Some days, the learning started even before I arrived at school. Like this morning, I was on the bus, when, at the stop after mine, this big guy got on, lumbered down to me, and said, "Hey, kid. This seat's taken."

"Of course it's taken," I agreed. "I'm sitting in it. But there's a vacant seat next to me. Feel free to use it."

"Beat it, nerd!" He picked me up by the collar and tossed me across the aisle. A moment later, my book bag slammed into my chest.

I was about to protest the rough treatment when I realized something: In my old seat, the window was open, and it was quite chilly outside. It wasn't a problem for him. He was a bigger, hardier person. So he wasn't being mean. He was doing me a favor.

When we were getting off the bus at school, I thanked him for his thoughtfulness. He stared at me and then looked up at the sky. So it *was* about the weather, as I'd suspected.

The social world at real school could be tricky to navigate. But the people were really nice, if only you took the time to understand them.

I still went to the Academy part-time. Donovan and I traveled together by minibus for robotics. But I wasn't that into it. Heavy Metal was a good robot, but any machine was, by definition, predictable. Every line of code in its computer software could be broken down; its hydraulic, pneumatic, and mechanical systems could be analyzed and understood. Any operation that didn't go exactly according to design could be traced to a specific malfunction—one that could be corrected and repaired. It was the opposite of YouTube, where, if you clicked on a video, you might get a kid on a pogo stick or a rocket launch at Cape Canaveral or some guy playing the piccolo with his nose or anything at all.

The best part of Heavy Metal was on the lower portion of the main body, just below the left lifting arm. I put it there myself. It was a picture of Tina Patterson taken at the hospital when she was only three hours old. Normally, Donovan was in charge of decorating our robot with images downloaded from the internet. So far, he had the flag of Namibia, an image of Abraham Lincoln with shades on, and a small poster that said: PANDAS ARE PEOPLE TOO. But my picture was better because nothing about Tina could ever be bad. And not even YouTube was as unpredictable as baby Tina. You never knew in advance if she was going to smile, scream, pass gas, gurgle, or spit up all over you. No one could be a know-it-all about Tina, not even me. She was a universal mystery, but that was okay. Whatever she did do, it was fine because her mom let me hold her. A lot.

In a way, Hardcastle Middle School was just as unpredictable as Tina, which was why I liked it so much. It was a lot more crowded than the Academy, so the hallways were chaotic, especially for a short person like me. That was another example of how the Academy, which was supposed to be so challenging, was much easier than here. Just getting from room to room without being elbowed, stepped on, or slammed into a wall was a learning experience. Sometimes Donovan or one of those two guys named Daniel would walk with me. That was something else I never had before—friends.

My favorite class—one that the Academy didn't offer—was gym. Of all the subjects where I had room for improvement, it was number one—even more than cooking. All phys ed classes were held in the old cafeteria, since the gymnasium we shared with Hardcastle High was being renovated after part of a broken statue bowled into it.

Gym had to be the happiest class in the whole school, always ringing with laughter—mostly when I tried to perform some physical skill. Except Donovan, come to think of it. He was always arguing with one of the guys or jumping in front of me, especially when we played dodgeball. Donovan was a terrible dodgeball player. He was constantly getting hit. Even when he'd already been eliminated, he would hurl himself between the ball and me, getting yelled at by players and earning lots of detentions from Coach Franco.

"You know, Donovan," I advised, trying to give back some of the loyalty and support I'd received from him since arriving here, "you really ought to chill out." That was one of his expressions. "And maybe you should practice dodgeball skills in your spare time. You're black-and-blue. Look at me. I didn't get hit once."

He clenched and unclenched his fists, which didn't seem like chilling out as I understood the term. Or maybe he was focusing on searching for my pants, which was kind of a gym class tradition. Whoever was picked last when we chose up teams got his pants hidden. I was really looking forward to the time when I could be in on the hiding part and not the finding at the end.

People were definitely different here compared to the Academy kids—louder, rougher, sometimes meaner. But I preferred it. People lived their lives here, instead of obsessing over grades or prizes or internships or getting into Stanford or Yale. You heard the phrase "Who cares?" at least fifty times a day. And a lot of those "Who cares?" kids had better grades than I did. What a thrill *that* was.

I was getting so good at mediocre academic performance that I was called to see Mrs. Ibrahimovic, my guidance counselor. She launched into a speech about how I had to try harder and attend extra help sessions because I was on the verge of failing some of my classes.

I got so emotional that I teared up. In my wildest dreams I never could have hoped that I, Noah Youkilis, would one day be in danger of flunking a subject.

"There's no need to cry," Mrs. Ibrahimovic said quickly. "There's still plenty of time before the end of the year. Don't give up hope."

I nodded, but I was still too emotional to manage any words.

"It's going to be all right," she soothed. "We'll get you the support you need. Let me take a look at the transcripts from your last school." She sifted through my folder and frowned at my records from the Academy, which told of my 206 IQ, my 100-percent average, and the scholarship offer I received from Princeton on my tenth birthday. "Well, this can't be right," she concluded, and put the file away. "Now listen, Noah, there's nothing to be so upset about. We'll put together a personalized study plan for you, and maybe consider some remedial classes."

I walked out of that office feeling ten feet tall.

Humming "Be True to Your School" under my breath, I paused in front of the big bulletin board outside guidance. What an awesome place this was! At the Academy, there wasn't a single extracurricular activity that I wouldn't automatically have been

27

number one at. Everything was different here. There was a golf team, a group that made quilts for residents of the local assisted living home, kids who volunteered at the animal shelter, a synchronized swimming club, rock climbers, coin collectors, a bluegrass band—it went on and on.

Giddy from my meeting with Mrs. Ibrahimovic, I felt an urge to join absolutely everything. But that was impossible. There weren't enough hours in the day.

My eyes fell on the very last poster on the board.

# CALLING ALL DANCERS
## THE LACROSSE TEAM NEEDS CHEERLEADERS
## CAN YOU BUST A MOVE AND RAISE THE ROOF?
## SCHOOL SPIRIT! EXERCISE! FUN!
## SUPPORT OUR HARDCASTLE HORNETS
## SIGN UP HERE

As soon as I saw it, I knew it was tailor-made for me. It was the words *school spirit* that put it over the top. *Be true to your school.* That's what I wanted to do—show this fantastic institution of learning how grateful I was for the opportunities it was giving me. And what better way to do that than by pledging my body and heart to supporting one of the sports teams.

As I signed my name on the dotted line, I'd never felt better about anything in my life.

Head held high, I started for the computer lab in the library. I didn't know anything about being a cheerleader, but I was sure there was a lot about it on YouTube.

In the hall, I passed Donovan.

"Hi, Noah," he said absently. Then he wheeled and grabbed my arm from behind. "Wait a minute—I don't like that look on your face. What are you up to?"

"I thought this year couldn't get any better," I told him. "How wrong a guy can be."

# 3

# SUPERCHEERFUL
## MEGAN MERCURY

*Two, four, six, eight, who do we appreciate? The seasons!*
Not fall, winter, spring, and summer. I meant football season, basketball season, and lacrosse season. The reason I left out soccer, wrestling, and baseball is that none of those sports had cheerleaders.

I was the head cheerleader of the Hardcastle squad—the only girl in school history ever to earn that position as a sixth grader and hold on to it for all three years. I wrote our cheers. I choreographed our routines. And when someone had to do a flip off the top of our human pyramid, that was me too.

I loved cheerleading because it was so positive. You cheer *for* something, not against it. We were even positive toward the opponents we were grinding into hamburger. Our squad always had a "Good effort!" or "We're proud of you, too!" I made sure of that.

I was in charge of everything, including recruiting. It was easy to fill out the squad for football season. Who didn't want to be a football cheerleader? It dropped off a little for basketball. But the season I really had to hold my breath for was lacrosse. It was an amazing sport, but it just didn't get the kind of buzz the others did. And I had to admit the guys could look pretty strange with all that bulky padding up top and skinny bare legs sticking out on the bottom.

We had a great team, though. We went all the way to regional finals last year, and this year the guys were confident they could make it to state. They deserved our support. They deserved the best cheerleading squad our school could put together.

So I was relieved when I approached the guidance office and saw that the sign-up sheet was at least half full.

Way to go, ladies!

Hash Taggart, our star midfielder, was standing at the bulletin board, checking out the names.

I flashed him thumbs-up and he responded with a confused expression.

"The squad," I said by way of explanation. "We must have at least nine or ten girls."

"Yeah, but who's"—Hashtag pointed to the last name on the list—"Noah Youkilis?"

I frowned. "Never heard of her. Maybe she's new."

"Isn't Noah a boy's name?"

"Not always," I replied. "I went to camp with a girl named Noah. But come to think of it, she spelled it without the *H*. I'll ask around. Somebody must know her."

I turned out to be wrong about that. Nobody knew a girl named Noah Youkilis. I asked all the other cheerleaders on the sheet and came up empty. Whoever she was, she didn't sign up with one of them.

I widened my search. There were nine hundred kids at our school, but I was pretty connected. If the head cheerleader wasn't at the center of things, who would be?

Hashtag was asking too, and he knew everybody. Or so I thought. He reported back to me: None of the guys had gone out with a girl named Noah. She wasn't anybody's kid sister. We were beginning to think that someone had put that name on the sign-up sheet as a hoax.

I began mentally choreographing routines for a nine-person squad, confident that the tenth name on our list was a ghost. And then one day, Daniel Nussbaum approached me, a goofy grin on his face.

"I hear you're looking for Noah Youkilis."

This wasn't a cheer-positive thought, but you didn't stay popular for three years by hanging out with the likes of Daniel Nussbaum. Still, I was sucked in by the possibility that the Youkilis mystery might have an actual solution. "You know her?"

The grin widened. "Yes and no. Follow me."

He led me to the old cafeteria, which we were using as a makeshift gym until the real gym was ready again. Coach Franco had set up an obstacle course, and there were kids all around the big room, tackling different athletic challenges.

Daniel elbowed me in the side and nodded in the direction of the vaulting horse, the first station in the course. This skinny, round-shouldered kid I didn't recognize burst over the starting tape, hit the springboard, and launched himself into the air. He got about an inch and a half off the floor and slammed face-first into the obstacle. He tried two more times before the coach took pity on the poor guy and boosted him to the top. But as he was crawling across it, he over-balanced and slid down the side to the mat.

"Go around it!" Coach Franco rasped.

"Wow," I breathed, watching as the kid tripped over every single tire he was supposed to run through in the next part of the course. "Who's that?"

Daniel beamed at me. "That would be Noah You-kilis."

"But"—I honestly thought my head might explode—"that's a *boy*."

"They have guy cheerleaders too, you know."

"Yeah, but *we* don't!"

He shot me a disapproving look. "That's sexist."

I was babbling. "I mean, we never had guys *before*. Why would he want to join an all-girls squad?"

"You and I might not be smart enough to under-stand. Noah Youkilis is *gifted*."

"What's his gift?" I demanded. "An internal gyro-scope set on random?"

Daniel laughed appreciatively. "Good one."

My stomach twisting, I watched Noah take on the rest of the course. He knocked over orange cones. He knocked over garbage cans. He even knocked over a couple of the guys who were trying to pass him from behind.

That wasn't the worst of it. Sure, he couldn't overcome the obstacles, but what was really horrifying was the way he ran between them—headlong, flailing, all four limbs moving in different directions. He looked like a spider that fell into the toilet and was swimming for his life.

Daniel was laughing now. "Lots of luck explaining *this* to the lacrosse team."

"This isn't over yet," I said grimly.

As I stormed through the halls, sixth graders scrambled to get out of my way. *Be positive,* I reminded myself. We cheerleaders were trained to keep smiles on our faces at all times—even if a meteor fell out of the sky and flattened the field in the middle of our routine.

But this was much more serious than that.

My destination: Ms. Torres, the cheerleading coach. She taught science for her regular job.

She left her class in the lab and I confronted her in the hall. "What's so important, Megan? There are seventh graders with Bunsen burners in there."

"Ms. Torres, someone named Noah Youkilis signed up for the lacrosse cheerleaders and—"

She held up her hand like a traffic cop. "Say no more. I know all about Noah. Just because we've never had male cheerleaders before doesn't mean they're not eligible. Those are the rules. Everybody is welcome to join any club or team. No exceptions."

"I don't care so much that it's a boy," I pleaded. "I care that it's *that* boy. He's the most uncoordinated person I've ever seen. He could never learn our routines."

I got the stop sign again. "That's enough. When I saw his name on the sheet, I went to see Noah. Not your typical eighth grader, I'll grant you. But I think he could be good for our squad."

"Good?" I choked. "How?"

"To be honest, when I met with him, I was planning on talking him out of it. Instead, he wound up talking me into it. He wants to be a cheerleader out of pure school spirit. That's something we don't see enough of these days. It might help some of the girls to cheer alongside someone who isn't just doing it for glory, attention, and a cute outfit."

That made me bristle. "No offense, Ms. Torres, but that's a little insulting. Some of us take cheerleading seriously. It's not about the outfit. I mean, the outfit *is* pretty cute . . ." I drifted off topic for a moment, thinking about our cheerleading costumes, which were perfection. Designed by me, of course. "Wait—what's he going to *wear*?"

She laughed. "Not the miniskirt, obviously. We'll keep it simple. Plain white pants, and white sneakers instead of those tasseled boots. I think the jacket will fit. He's not very muscular."

Understatement of the century. Noah had arms like bent coat hangers and shoulders the width of a fire hydrant. Next to all those top-heavy lacrosse guys, he was going to look like a string bean with Coke-bottle glasses.

"Everybody's going to laugh at us," I predicted mournfully.

Her expression turned disapproving. "You've just illustrated exactly why we need Noah on our squad. It's fine to impress people, but it's not fine when you start trying to weed out the people you don't think are impressive enough. If you're such a good choreographer, develop a routine that suits his style."

"His style is falling down and wiping out everybody around him," I protested.

One thing about Ms. Torres—she expressed her anger by becoming extra quiet. "Well, Megan, if you can't hack it, I'll accept your resignation as head cheerleader."

That shocked me a little, but I kept my cool. There was no way Ms. Torres was going to kick me out. I was the best cheerleader to come around this place since the legendary squad that inspired me to become a cheerleader in the first place. It would take a lot more than Noah Youkilis to change that.

*Stay positive,* I coached myself. I wasn't anti-Noah; I was pro-squad. Which meant I couldn't let that clumsy little twerp make us look like idiots in front of every lacrosse fan in the county.

It was time to bring out the heavy artillery.

# 4

# SUPERATHLETE
## HASH TAGGART

**M**egan Mercury just didn't get it. Nobody went to a lacrosse game to watch the *cheerleaders*. When it came to sports, *I* was the authority, not any pom-pom girl. Not only was I the star middie at lax, but I also quarterbacked the football team. At wrestling I didn't hold any specific role. I was just a beast.

So when Megan came to me in full freak-out mode, blubbering about some dude named Noah who wanted to join the cheerleaders, my reaction was, "Chill out,

Megan. I mean, stinks to be you. But what am I supposed to do about it?"

Until I got a load of this Youkilis kid at the big pep rally. We held it in the cafeteria because there was still no gym. Coach Franco introduced the team first. The players got a pretty good ovation, especially me. Then the cheerleaders came out. There was the standard hooting mixed with the usual buzzing of a few idiots who barely knew what they were there for.

Noah came on last. I'd seen plenty of guy cheerleaders. Trust me, this was different. It was impossible to come up with only one word to describe the kid. He was like a dweeb/shrimp/goober/stick-bug/klutz. When he first shambled out, total silence greeted his arrival. Then as the crowd began to realize that they were actually seeing what they thought they were seeing, a wave of laughter and cheers began to rise.

Thinking this was a welcoming ovation, Noah took a deep bow, bonking his head on our team flagpole, knocking it over into the front row of seats. Kids scattered in all directions.

Now Noah really did get an ovation—a standing one. People were practically losing their minds and screaming their heads off.

I thought back to Megan's words: *Believe me, Hashtag,*

*no one's going to notice there's a team on the field once that train wreck gets going!*

She was right. Here we were, center stage, in our own cafeteria, in front of our own fans, and nobody was even looking at us. All eyes were on the train wreck, who was jumping around like someone had put ten thousand volts through him, waving to the crowd with one hand, and holding his rapidly swelling forehead with the other.

If this kid stayed on the cheerleading squad, this wouldn't be a lacrosse season; it would be a sketch on *Saturday Night Live.* In sports, if you're not respected, you can't be feared. And it's impossible to be feared if your opponents are too busy laughing at the dweeb/shrimp/goober/stick-bug/klutz in the cheerleading suit.

So I made a mental note to have a little conversation with this Youkilis kid to discuss his cheerleading future, and the fact that he wasn't going to have one. At first, I staked out the girls' locker room, because that's where the cheerleaders change.

Megan set me straight when she came out in her street clothes. "Of course he doesn't dress in here with *us!* He's in the *guys'* locker room!"

That was even worse. It meant he'd be with the team.

Not only would we be stuck with him on the field; *every* game would start with a little preview of dweeb/shrimp/goober/stick-bug/klutz. No one would be able to pay attention to Coach Franco. I was more convinced than ever that Youkilis had to go—for the good of the Hornets.

So I waited outside the guys' room. Five minutes. Then ten. No dweeb/shrimp/goober/stick-bug/klutz. Finally, I decided I'd better go in just in case he'd flushed himself down the toilet and needed a lifeguard.

He was there all right, running around in his underwear, peering into lockers and bins.

"What's the problem?" I asked him.

"Oh, hi," he said to me. "You wouldn't happen to know where my pants are, would you?"

I looked up and there they were, right where I expected them to be—draped over the blades of the ceiling fan, turning slowly. I reached up, grabbed a dangling leg, pulled them down, and tossed them to their owner.

"Get dressed," I told him, looking away because those pale skinny legs were burning my eyes. "We have to talk about how you don't want to be a cheerleader anymore."

"But I *do*!" he exclaimed, stepping into his jeans—and then out again so he could put them on the right way. "It's the least I can do to be true to my school."

He must have been a great actor, because I could have sworn he was sincere. "All right, kid, I'm not brain dead. What are you trying to prove?"

"Prove?" He frowned. "You can prove a mathematical equation by demonstrating it holds true for any of a domain of numbers, but I don't see how that concept applies to cheerleading."

My eyes narrowed. "What are you, a wise guy?"

"I used to be," he admitted. "I'm an average student now. I might even get to take remedial classes."

I breathed a silent apology to Megan. Noah Youkilis was the most annoying person who ever stumbled across the face of the earth. He was obviously messing with me, calling me stupid or something. I didn't take that from anybody.

I grabbed him under his arms and lifted him off the floor. I couldn't help noticing that both his feet were sticking out of one pant leg. This clown had the nerve to insult *me*, the captain of three sports teams. "Hang up your pom-poms, little man," I told him. "You're done." And I walked out of there, leaving him to find his second pant leg all by himself.

Before the door eased itself shut behind me, I heard him say, "There are no loops to hang them by. It's a design flaw."

The next day, when I jogged out onto the field for lax practice, I glanced over to the sidelines where the cheerleaders were working out and I couldn't believe my eyes. It was Noah! I thought I'd been speaking English yesterday, not Swahili. I had made my message 1000 percent clear!

Megan shot me an accusing look, like I'd epically failed at my assignment. Actually, she was right.

I ran over, pulled him out of formation, and hissed, "What are you doing here?"

He beamed at me and held out one of his pom-poms. "Look. I've installed a loop of elastic fabric, affixed with industrial staples, so it can hang from any peg or hook. I told the girls it was your idea." He tried to wink, but he couldn't even get that right, blinking both eyes.

I swear, I just stood there with my mouth hanging open. I might still be there if Coach Franco hadn't blown his whistle to get started.

Practice was terrible. The other players were okay, but I just couldn't get my act together. It's impossible to throw and catch with a lax stick unless your head is in the game. And if I was off, all the guys were off, because every play went through me at some point. Coach Franco practically passed out from blowing his whistle so often.

He had a lot of suggestions about what we needed to do to improve. I didn't listen to any of them. I knew that what really needed to improve was the Youkilis situation.

I kept an eye out for Noah around school, staking out his locker, cornering him in the lunchroom. "You haven't quit yet! That better be because you've got laryngitis, so you've got no voice to tell Megan the bad news."

"Oh, no, my voice is exemplary," he replied cheerfully. "A fine thing that would be—a cheerleader who can't cheer."

"That's what I'm trying to tell you," I insisted. "You can't cheer. It's over."

"On the contrary, the season hasn't even started yet."

"Listen, man, this is a cheerleading squad *not* including you. You're not on it."

"Certainly, I'm on it. I'll show you the list."

"I know you're *on* it, but you're *off* it!"

"That," he informed me, "is a logical impossibility."

I was getting more ticked off every day. So was Megan. Not at him. At *me*!

"I don't want to be negative, but he's ruining our routines!" She was trying to remain calm, but I could sense her anger crackling under the surface. "When everybody else turns left, he turns right. We're in tight formation, and he's all over the place. He measured our human pyramid with a protractor! He translated our fight song into Latin! You've got to do something!"

"So how's that my problem?" I shot back. "*You're* the head cheerleader! Kick him off the squad."

"Ms. Torres won't let me. She says he has more school spirit than the rest of us put together. For some reason, she's protecting him."

"*Protecting* him?" I echoed. "He doesn't need protection! The kid's an alien, sent down from the mothership to drive everybody crazy. We need protection from *him*!"

"Oh, come on!" she exploded. "Some tough guy you are. Stop giving the guy supernatural powers. He's not an alien; he's just plain clueless. Stop being so subtle! You're going to have to get right in his face and tell him how it is."

I agonized over that. Noah Youkilis had become almost an obsession. He was so far inside my head that

I couldn't do things on the lacrosse field that were practically second nature to me. I saw his eager goofball grin in my sleep. Was it possible that he wasn't evil at all—that he simply didn't understand what I was telling him?

The more I thought about it, the more sense it made. You couldn't lean on a guy who barely had the sense to notice he was being leaned on. I had to threaten him, pure and simple. I'd already told him to quit the cheerleaders. What I hadn't said was quit the cheerleaders *or else*. Two extra words that made all the difference.

It would be an ugly scene, but it would be worth it. Youkilis would be gone once and for all, and then the Hornets could get back to lacrosse.

But I couldn't risk confronting him at school. There was too great a chance of being overheard by one of the teachers. Coach Franco had a zero-tolerance policy on bullying. If you got caught, you were off the team. Even if you were only doing it out of team spirit.

No, this had to be done outside of school. Hardcastle was a small town. Noah couldn't hide forever.

# 5

# SUPERSCUFFLE
## DONOVAN CURTIS

Kandy had a playdate on Saturday. His sister, Marie
Curie, was visiting. Chloe Garfinkle, Marie's
owner, was on the robotics team with Noah and
me. Chloe went to the Academy full-time, like Noah
should have, and I used to, by mistake.

Marie Curie was already housebroken, which was
a lot more than I could say for our Kandahar, who
was still dribbling—and worse—all over the carpet.
Marie had a nice quiet chew toy, not that instrument

of torture, the bowwow bone. She was better-looking than Kandy, too. She had been spared the enormous feet of the absentee father, so she could cross a room without tripping. She was definitely smarter—and not just because she was named after a famous scientist. I experienced a pang of guilt for thinking bad things about Kandy. He might have been an ugly, untrainable, mongrel, but he was my ugly, untrainable mongrel.

The two pups rolled around the backyard and seemed to have a good time together. It was a great reunion— much better than Marie's with her mother, Beatrice, who ignored her like she wasn't there. The cinnamon chow chow was sulking because Brad wasn't paying any attention to her. He was walking up and down with a fussy baby Tina, trying to keep her quiet while my sister napped upstairs.

Brad's back was straight as a telephone pole, his posture upright, his free arm swinging in a controlled arc at his side. His other arm supported his daughter as if she was a rifle and he was marching in tight military formation.

"Come on, Tina. Naptime means lights-out for you. This fussing isn't regulation."

Chloe had a suggestion. The Academy kids always did. "Your posture's too good."

My brother-in-law frowned. "Too *good*?"

"It's *motion* that soothes a crying baby," Chloe explained. "Your body position is so straight that poor Tina might as well be standing still. Try slouching a little."

The tank commander looked completely blank.

"You know," she added, "walk like Donovan."

Brad examined me a moment, and then rounded his shoulders, unstraightened his back, and allowed his head to droop a little. The change in his gait had Tina bobbing with every step. She quieted almost immediately, lolling against her father's chest. Within seconds, she was fast asleep. Brad tossed a whispered "Thanks!" over his shoulder.

"I slump like that?" I asked Chloe.

She shrugged. "No kid has the carriage of a Marine officer."

"You didn't answer my question," I said, slightly miffed.

In spite of everything, I was glad to see Chloe. I saw her a lot at the Academy, but then it was always robotics business. Heavy Metal was really taking shape. Latrell, who did most of our hands-on metal work, had completed the stainless steel body, so we were way ahead of schedule. Getting the new robot ready was our goal for the rest of this semester, but he wouldn't be going into competition until next year, when we'd be freshmen in high school.

"How's Noah doing?" Chloe wanted to know. As smart as Noah was, she always felt protective of him.

"Depends who you talk to," I told her. "If you go by Noah, he's doing amazing. He got his first D last week, and his counselor is threatening to put him in remedial classes."

She shook her head in exasperation. "Don't they understand how brilliant he is?"

"He's too brilliant for anybody to understand," I replied. "Least of all me. I can't even paper-train a baby dog."

"They're called puppies," she reminded me. She seemed worried. "Noah told Abigail he joined the *cheerleading squad*. That can't be right, can it?"

"He's number one at everything, for thirteen years. Now he's determined to do everything he's bad at. Cheerleading might be his crowning achievement."

She picked up Marie, who had fallen asleep on the grass. "When you think about it," she said with a sigh, "it can't really hurt him. He's Noah. Even if he flunks the whole year, he can teach himself everything he missed in two weeks."

Suddenly, the sprinkler system burst to life, drenching everyone with a fine shower of water. We all scattered.

"What the—?" Brad turned his back to protect Tina from the spray. It was too late. The baby was bawling from the shock of the cold drops on her face.

Only Kandy stood there, bewildered, gazing around in wonder, his big ears dripping.

We looked to the sprinkler controls. Beatrice still had the tap in her teeth, a defiant expression in her brown eyes.

Brad used to think it was clever that Beatrice had figured out how to turn on the sprinklers when she wanted a drink. Now he was furious. "Bad dog!" he shouted.

It only made Tina cry harder. There was nothing wrong with that kid's lungs.

The upstairs window opened and Katie stuck her head out, her nap interrupted. "What's going on?"

That was enough to draw my mother into the conversation. She stormed out on the back porch. "*Donnie!*"

That was what passed for math at our house. Brad's dog + Brad and Katie's daughter + our sprinklers = *my* fault.

I caught a quizzical glance from Chloe, which told

me that her 159 IQ couldn't figure it out either.

I pointed to Beatrice at the tap. "It was *her*!"

"Take the dog for a walk!" Mom ordered.

"Why me?" I demanded. "She's Brad's dog!"

"In the Corps," my brother-in-law lectured, "we do what needs to be done, and everybody pulls their own weight."

It was never good news when Brad began a sentence with "In the Corps . . ." For sure, he'd be about to make another comparison between the real world and the Marines, where reality just didn't measure up. As much as he loved his family, he really missed military life. I almost felt bad for him—except that I was the part of the real world that didn't measure up the most.

"We're all taking on a little extra responsibility these days, Donnie," my mother added from the window. "It wouldn't kill you to pitch in."

So Kandy went back inside, and I took Beatrice out on the leash. Chloe and Marie Curie walked with us for a while.

Chloe tried to make me feel better. "It's basic psychology. Beatrice is acting up because she's jealous of the new baby."

Chloe had some kind of scientific theory for everything.

"It doesn't explain everything," I grumbled. "Brad is out to turn me into a junior marine. If he doesn't get redeployed soon, I'm going to have to find a new family."

Chloe and Marie Curie turned off on Zinnia Street, and Beatrice and I continued to the park. Beatrice was calmer now that Brad and Tina were out of her line of vision. Score one for science.

"Hang in there, girl," I said to the dog. "One of these days you're going to like Tina. We'll bring her to the playground together." My eyes found the jungle gym—the little kids swarming over the equipment.

That was when I noticed that one of the little kids wasn't a little kid at all. He was a big kid who just happened to be little. It was Noah, and he was throwing himself around in the wood chips that surrounded the climbing apparatus and slides. Why was he hurling himself to the ground like that, his arms and legs splayed out wide like he was a starfish or something? It took a while, but I figured out what he was up to. Hardcastle's newest cheerleader was trying to teach himself to do a cartwheel. And Noah being Noah, it wasn't going very well.

All at once, a burly muscular kid on a bicycle came tearing into the playground, stopping with the front tire half an inch from Noah's belly button. Then the big guy was down off the bike, hauling Noah up by his shirt.

"Hey!" I was on the run toward them, Beatrice loping at my side. It was the kind of bullying I'd been on high alert for since Noah's day one at our school, but that had never quite materialized beyond a few snide comments and a sudden burst of enthusiasm for dodgeball in gym class.

I recognized the kid—Hash Taggart, who was kind of the über-jock at Hardcastle Middle. He wrestled Noah to the ground and straddled him, a knee pinning each arm. They were pretty loud, too—the lacrosse star's booming voice and Noah's answering squeaks.

"I gave you a million chances to back off!" Hashtag was raving. "An imbecile could have figured it out!"

"Are you sure?" Noah replied seriously. "An imbecile has an IQ between twenty-six and fifty. My IQ has been measured at two hundred and six—"

"Shut up!" Hashtag bellowed. "I'm not listening to you! You make people crazy!"

"—although of course these days the idea that IQ tests provide a true measure of intelligence is considered fundamentally flawed—"

"Shut up!" Hashtag bellowed. He drew back a meaty fist, about to pulverize skinny Noah.

I left my feet in a desperation dive and tackled Hashtag. It hurt like mad when my nose slammed into his shoulder, but not as much as when I slid through the wood chips, picking up splinters over at least half my body.

Hashtag turned his attention away from Noah and onto me. Sure, he was five times bigger than Noah, but he was still at least twice the size of me. Funny that I should only consider that when it was too late. It was my fallout blindness the Daniels found so entertaining. I was great at taking action, but not so great at thinking about the consequences first.

"Curtis?" he roared, springing back to his feet.

"Pick on someone your own size!" I shot back, which was probably stupid because there weren't any sumo wrestlers in our neighborhood.

And then his fist was coming at me. It made contact with the side of my face, and everything went gray.

The next thing I heard was a bark of outrage, and a cinnamon-brown bundle of fur was airborne. Her jaws clamped onto the arm of Hashtag's windbreaker.

The lacrosse star let out a scream that easily eclipsed anything that had come out of either Noah or me.

"Beatrice! Let go!" To be honest, I was kind of stunned that the chow chow would go to war for me.

She hung on like a crocodile.

"Bad dog!" I scolded.

*"Bad?"* Hashtag howled, trying in vain to shake his arm free. "That's the best you can do? How about 'nightmare hound from the deepest, darkest . . .'"

He went on and on, scaring the little kids, and—worse—attracting the attention of their parents. Not good.

What could I do? I took out my phone and called Brad.

First Lieutenant Bradley Patterson, United States Marine Corps, came running in a full-on sprint to his chow chow's side.

By the time he arrived on the scene, Hashtag's parents were already there. "Are you the owner?" Hashtag's father demanded.

"Yes, sir. Bradley Patterson—"

Mr. Taggart cut him off. "I'm a volunteer fireman, so I know what happens to pets that pose a danger to the public. First, the dog is quarantined by Animal Control to check if it has rabies—"

"I assure you that Beatrice doesn't have rabies," Brad

put in fervently. "She's up-to-date on all her shots."

"Second," Hashtag's dad went on as if no one had spoken, "there's a hearing to determine if it should be declared vicious and put down."

"The technical term is *euthanized*," Noah supplied helpfully.

All color drained from Brad's face. You could even see it underneath his Marine Corps buzz cut. This was a guy who drove a tank through hostile territory for a living. But the thought of anything happening to Beatrice turned him to jelly.

To be honest, I wasn't too thrilled about that part myself. If I hadn't tried to save Noah, Hashtag wouldn't have punched me, and Beatrice wouldn't have bitten anybody. It was my fallout blindness coming back to haunt me. Only this time, the fallout wouldn't be coming down on me. Brad's dog might be the one to pay the price.

"Hashtag started it," I exclaimed angrily. "He was pushing Noah around. And when I tried to get him to stop, he practically knocked my head off."

"Let's see what Animal Control has to say about it," Mr. Taggart replied smugly.

"Mind if I have a word with my brother-in-law for a second?" Brad put an iron arm around my shoulders and steered me away from the Taggarts.

I was still speaking up for Beatrice. *"That's* the only reason Beatrice bit him! She was protecting *me* —"

*"Quiet!"* he hissed. "Beatrice can't go before a hearing."

"But she's *innocent—*"

"Listen! Back when Beatrice was with my mother, there was an incident. These kids were playing Frisbee, and one of them ran into her and knocked her over. Well, Beatrice thought it was an attack—"

"She bit someone else too?" Well, what did you know? Beatrice had a *past*. She was a criminal—and a repeat offender, no less.

Brad's speech was clipped. *"Don't. Say. The B-word.* So whatever we do, we can't let this go before Animal Control."

"Yeah, but how can we stop it?" I asked in a low voice. "Mr. Taggart's almost as big a jerk as his kid."

"We apologize," he whispered. *"You* apologize."

"For what?" I demanded. "Smashing my face into his delicate little fist?"

Brad ignored my protest and dragged me back to the Taggarts.

Hashtag's mom was taking pictures of her son's injured arm—probably evidence to use in doggie court or whatever. There were teeth marks and swelling, but the skin was unbroken.

"That's good news," Noah offered wisely. "It's impossible for rabies to be transmitted unless there's blood."

"Since when are you the big expert?" Hashtag exploded. "It really hurts! What if I can't play lacrosse? You need forearm strength, you know!"

"There's no rabies, I promise," Brad insisted.

"Even so," Mr. Taggart countered, "you can see how hard this is on a sensitive boy."

"Yeah"—it just slipped out—"Hashtag looked real sensitive while he was getting ready to beat the snot out of Noah."

If looks could kill, the one I got from Brad would have vaporized me as surely as a shot from his M1 tank.

Mrs. Taggart wasn't too pleased either. "We could sue."

"You could," Noah agreed, "but you wouldn't get much. I don't think tank commanders make a lot of money."

"Tank commanders?" Hashtag's father looked at Brad in surprise. "You're a military man?"

Brad stood up even straighter than his usual ramrod

posture. "Marine Corps, sir. On furlough between tours in Afghanistan."

Mr. Taggart was impressed. "Really? I was Army myself—quartermaster corps. Never saw any action, though—unless you count the time the women's barracks ran out of shampoo." He reached out a hand. "Thank you for your service."

I didn't think my brother-in-law would be too anxious to shake hands with someone who'd threatened to have Beatrice put down. But he swallowed his pride and pumped the man's arm.

Hashtag chimed in. "But we're still calling the cops on the mutt, right?"

"Mutt is an erroneous term," Noah corrected him. "It refers to a mixed breed, while Beatrice is a purebred chow chow."

"Kid, do you *ever* shut up?"

"Not when I have something informative to offer" was Noah's response.

"Let's just chalk this up as an unfortunate incident," Mr. Taggart decided. "I'd hate to make trouble for one of our brave fighting men."

I could see Brad relax. "I appreciate that, sir."

"But I don't want that dog anywhere near my son," Hashtag's mother warned, "or we *will* have her declared vicious. Don't think we won't." She glared at me. "And you stay away too."

And that was it. Beatrice was off the hook. Brad was off the hook. Even Noah was off the hook. Mr. Taggart gave his son a lecture about "picking on a little guy."

The only person who wasn't off the hook? Me.

"I'm not going to forget about this, Curtis," Hashtag whispered. "That shot in the face—consider it a down payment."

If that wasn't bad enough, Brad blamed me for the whole thing. "I asked you to do one thing, Donnie: take Beatrice for a walk. I guess that was too hard for you."

"What was I supposed to do?" I protested. "Let Hashtag pummel Noah?"

"There you go again," my brother-in-law accused. "Nothing is ever your fault. There's always some excuse."

"But it really *is* an excuse!" I protested.

"Now you're making an excuse about an excuse," he snapped. "Listen, Donovan, I see you roll your eyes when I talk about the military life. But it's not all about tanks and weapons systems and combat. It's about the kind of person you're going to be—having high standards for yourself and living by a code of honor, integrity, and discipline."

"If this is about me getting a buzz cut," I interjected, "I don't want to hear it."

"The haircut is just a symbol. It's a token of your commitment to be a part of something greater than yourself."

"I have enough trouble just being me," I retorted. "Didn't you notice that a three-sport varsity athlete almost took my head off back there?"

He frowned. "Fine. I'm just some jarhead marine to you. I don't care about that. But if you screw up, you put Beatrice in danger. You are going to stay away from that Hashtag. You don't fight with him; you don't talk to him; you don't even breathe the air in his zip code."

"But how can I help it if he comes after me?" I appealed.

"That's your problem, Donnie. Whatever happens to Beatrice is on your head. If she suffers, you suffer. Is that clear?"

Hey, this was a guy who made his living blowing stuff up with his tank and driving over the wreckage. And the next wreckage might be me.

Was it clear? You bet.

# 6

## SUPERLOYAL
### NOAH YOUKILIS

The lacrosse field resounded with the roar of the crowd, the referees' whistles, and the shouts of the players. I was really doing it—cheerleading— and it was the greatest experience of my life.

There could be no more amazing sport than lacrosse, which combined all the best elements of the other sports. The ball was baseball-ish, the pads were football-ish, the nets were hockey-ish, the cleats were soccer-ish, the shorts were basketball-ish, and the sticks were kind of butterfly–nettish, because they had little webbed pouches for passing and catching. With all it had to offer, I couldn't understand why lacrosse wasn't the national pastime. On YouTube, which was normally so sensible, there were far fewer lacrosse videos than all those inferior sports. I guess even YouTube could fall short every once in a while.

The only thing better than lacrosse was cheerleading for it. I only got injured once, when the integrity of my cartwheel disintegrated. As I collapsed, my foot slammed into something hard, and I experienced sharp pain in three of five metatarsals.

But I carried on bravely. The loud *"Ow!"* came not from me, but from Vanessa Mulcair, whose face turned out to be the something hard I'd injured my metatarsals on.

"Will you get a clue?" Megan yelled at me. As head cheerleader, it was her job to provide helpful coaching while the game was going on.

There was this YouTube video called "Playing through Pain" that inspired me to ignore my throbbing foot and cheer louder, even when my throat began to hurt worse than my toes. In the world of sports, this was known as "giving 110 percent," although that was a mathematical impossibility.

When the clock ran out, I jumped for joy, throwing my pom-poms in the air—although they didn't go very high.

Megan, our captain, turned furious eyes on me. "Shut up! Everyone will think we're nuts!"

I was mystified. "We're cheerleaders. It's our job to lead the cheers for our glorious victory."

"We didn't have a glorious victory! Can't you read a scoreboard?"

"Indeed I can," I replied. "When your team scores a plurality of goals, you win. Arithmetic dictates that fifteen is greater than three. Therefore, we are the winners." I almost added *quod erat demonstrandum*, but I remembered at the last minute that Latin wasn't too popular in the cheerleading business.

Megan's face was a thundercloud. "Only we didn't have the fifteen. We had the three."

"But it says *H* for Hornets!"

The look she gave me would have melted steel. "*H* is for home, not Hornets. We're the *visitors,* Noah. The *V* number."

Obviously, there was a lot more to cheerleading than I'd previously thought. It certainly explained why the girls had seemed so subdued on the sidelines.

On the bus back to school, I apologized to my fellow

cheerleaders. "I'm researching this whole home/visitors thing. I'll get it right next time."

"Next time," repeated Vanessa, holding the ice pack to her cheek.

The only other boy on the bus was Hash Taggart, with his arm in a sling. He couldn't play today, so he didn't have to stick around for Coach Franco's postgame session.

For some reason, he told everyone that his injury came from getting his arm caught in a car door.

"No, it didn't," I told him. "You were bitten by a dog."

"It was a car door," he said between clenched teeth.

"It was Beatrice. Don't you remember? She attacked you for punching Donovan Curtis."

"Curtis!" Hashtag practically spat. "This is all his fault! I'm going to get back at that guy if it's the last thing I do."

People always said that the Academy was much harder than Hardcastle Middle School, but this was a perfect illustration of why they were wrong. This situation couldn't be solved like an equation. It required a higher level of analysis—social analysis:

(1) Hashtag wasn't threatening me at all. He liked me. Everybody did. But (2) I owed it to Donovan to

warn him that the captain of the lacrosse team had it out for him. Because (3) when you had friends, you had to be loyal to them, even when it wasn't your problem.

Thus (4), what I said to Donovan at school the next morning:

"Hashtag is going to get even with you," I told him. "I don't think you have to worry about it right away, though. He said it's going to be the last thing he does."

Donovan sighed. "Yeah, I kind of figured what happened in the park wasn't over yet. Especially when I heard that he might be out for the whole lacrosse season."

"What are you going to do?" I asked.

A shrug. "I'll steer clear of the guy. He's just a bully. Not much else I can do."

"I once saw a YouTube video called 'Stand Up to Bullies.'"

He shook his head. "Not an option. Hashtag's parents have pictures of the bite marks on his arm, and Mrs. Taggart pretty much threatened to report Beatrice to Animal Control. If there's another scrape between Hashtag and me, you can take that to the bank."

I could see it was a real dilemma for poor Donovan. He was being wronged, but he couldn't take action to right that wrong without putting Beatrice's life in danger.

Then something strange happened. When I solved an impossible math problem or came up with a flaw-less argument for an English essay or explained an anomaly in a chemistry experiment, it was always the easiest, most natural thing in the world, like flicking a bug off your arm. This was different. When I came up with the solution, it was completely unexpected, a sudden sunrise over a mountain range, a brainstorm.

"I'll do it for you!" I exclaimed.

"Do what for me?" he asked.

"You can't stand up to Hashtag because of Beatrice," I exclaimed breathlessly. "But *I* can!"

Donovan laughed in my face. "Don't be crazy. He'll kill you."

"He would *today*," I agreed. "That's why it's a good thing we have plenty of time. I intend to use mine wisely."

His eyes narrowed. "Wisely how?"

"The key to any confrontation is having the best strategy."

"No," he told me, "the key is a hard right to the head." He rubbed his jaw, which was still a little bruised. "Hashtag has it. I'm living proof of that. You don't want to join the club."

"When the time comes," I promised, "I'll be ready. I'll tell Hashtag that he better not be mean to my friend Donovan. It'll be just like 'Stand Up to Bullies.'"

He grabbed my arm. "Cut it out, Noah. This kid could do a lot of damage without even meaning to hurt you very much. Promise me you'll stay away from him."

I could tell he was 100 percent serious. He wasn't going to let me go until I gave him my word.

"I promise," I lied.

Lying was another excellent skill I'd picked up since coming to Hardcastle Middle. There hadn't been much call for it at the Academy, but here you could make use of it dozens of times every day. For example, when somebody confronted you with, "Hey, dork, are you looking at me?" it was generally better to say no.

Or in this case, where I lied because I didn't want Donovan to worry about me. I'd be fine. Before confronting Hashtag, I would learn the art of self-defense from the greatest gladiators the world had ever known—WWE wrestlers. And I knew exactly where to find them: in the same place all the true secrets of humanity are just waiting to be accessed.

YouTube.

\* \* \*

My YouTube search for keyword *WWE* yielded over thirteen million hits. With an average length of over four minutes per video, I obviously wouldn't be able to watch them all. But I was able to see enough to learn how to handle myself if things got ugly with Hashtag.

The average wrestler was six foot four and two hundred fifty pounds. I wasn't going to be able to bulk up to that level on such short notice. So I zeroed in on the concepts that applied to everybody—speed, explosiveness, focus, muscle power, and the element of surprise. There were important moves to be mastered—chokeslams, piledrivers, sleeper holds, spinebusters, clotheslines, and frog splashes. Also, it never hurt to have a steel folding chair handy just in case you had to break it over somebody's head.

Every day after cheerleading practice, I'd rush home and spend hours in front of the computer, drinking it all in. At night, when I was supposed to be sleeping, I practiced against my pillow. Once, while taking out the garbage, I powerbombed a green bag. It exploded, sending chicken bones and orange peels all over the lawn. My mother said our property smelled like the town dump, but to me it smelled like victory. And anyway, she helped me clean it up, so it only cost me forty-five minutes of YouTube research.

I considered the best place to make my move on Hashtag. School had its advantages—for one thing, there were always a lot of chairs around. But also a lot of people. Too many, in fact. No, this had to happen somewhere more private.

I didn't know where he lived, but that was no problem. I hacked into the school computer and got his address—42 Staunton Street, about half a mile away from my house. I calculated that the optimal time would be early Saturday morning, around seven a.m., when most people would still be in bed.

Once my plan was set, keeping my excitement to myself was almost more than I could bear. I was dying to tell someone about it, but the only person I could think of was Donovan. And the whole reason for the lie was to keep him in the dark.

I woke up at five-thirty that morning with great singleness of purpose. I had my outfit all set. Unfortunately, I couldn't find my Speedo, so I substituted long underwear from when I was eight—super-tight, very WWE. Up top, I wore a sweatshirt that I'd carefully cut open with a pair of scissors, so it was only closed by a few threads. It took me hours, but it was totally worth it. If Hashtag got physical, I could tear it off in a heartbeat, just like the real superstars did. Since I had no wrestling gloves, I substituted the gloves Mom used for gardening. I tried to cut off the fingertips, but the fabric was really thick. On my feet I wore patent leather dress shoes, but I blackened the bottom of my long underwear with spray paint, so it would look like boots.

I was ready by 5:45, so I had to cool my heels for a while. If I got there too early, Hashtag might still be in bed, and maybe his parents wouldn't want to disturb him.

At 6:45, Mom and Dad were sleeping when I tip-toed downstairs and eased myself outside, careful not to bang the folding chair under my arm against the storm door. Jackpot! The neighborhood was deserted: no kids outside playing, no parents around.

All the way from my house to Staunton Street the only sign of life was a single car. It drove past me, screeched to a halt, then backed up. The rear door opened and one of those kids named Daniel jumped out—I never could tell the two of them apart.

"Noah, is that you?" he demanded. "Why are you dressed like that?"

"I could ask you the same question," I retorted. He

was in a suit and tie. He had no chair, obviously—not unless the seats in the car counted.

"We're on our way to my cousin's bar mitzvah," he explained. "Where are you going so early? And what's up with the folding chair?"

I hesitated. This was supposed to be top secret. "I'm a morning person," I told him. "I'm just—taking a walk. The chair is in case I get tired."

"Don't give me that! What are you up to?"

"Nothing," I said casually, but he didn't seem convinced.

"Come on, Daniel," came a woman's voice from the car. "We're going to be late."

"Yeah, Mom, but remember when I told you about this kid—"

"*Now!*" It definitely wasn't a suggestion.

He got back in the car. Even as they drove away, I could see him, face pressed against the window, staring at me. They disappeared down the road, turning toward the highway.

I breathed a sigh of relief.

My plan was still on.

# 7

# SUPERHERO
## DONOVAN CURTIS

For a surefire alarm clock, you couldn't do much better than dog slobber.

"Cut it out, Beatrice," I complained, burying my head deeper into my pillow to avoid the chow chow's slimy tongue.

It did the trick—for about thirty seconds. The next thing I knew, I felt a strange buzzing against the back of my neck, pulsing on and off like—

"My phone?"

I flipped over in bed, dislodging my cell phone from the dog's mouth. It was set on mute, but there was no mistaking the vibration of an incoming call.

Who could be trying to reach me *now*? Which of my friends would even be awake at—I blinked the sleep out of my eyes and stared at the lit-up screen—6:52 on a Saturday morning?

I squinted to bring the caller ID into focus: *DANIEL N.*

Nussbaum.

I snatched up the unit, wiped the drool off on my comforter, and mumbled, "What?"

"Donovan—are you asleep?"

"Yeah." My reply was bitter. "I'm right in the middle of a bad dream about some idiot waking me up at the crack of dawn."

"Listen, I just saw Noah."

"And I should care about this because . . . ?" I prompted with a yawn.

"He was dressed all funny in, like, thermal ballet tights, and—forget it. I'll never describe it right. And he had a chair—"

"A *chair*?"

"—and that look on his face. You know, the one where he's about do something dumber than usual—?"

Noah's IQ was actually higher than the two Daniels' put together, with mine thrown in for good measure, but I let it pass. "I thought you and Sanderson were done looking out for Noah," I interrupted. "It was too much of a hit on your image, remember?"

"We *were*! It's just that—well, he was just starting down Staunton Street."

"So?"

"So isn't that where Hashtag lives?"

The pieces fell into place with a painful clunk. The world's greatest genius was making good on his promise to stand up to my bully for me—after I specifically made him swear he wouldn't! The ballet tights and the chair were a little confusing. But, hey, this was Noah. There didn't have to be a reason! And if he showed up on the Taggarts' doorstep at this hour to fight with Hashtag, what was left of him would be delivered to his parents in an eyedropper!

"I'm on it!" I wheezed at the phone and broke the connection. I leaped out of bed and threw on jeans and a shirt. Kandy was asleep in his usual position—on his back with his giant paws splayed in all directions. But Beatrice was watching me in keen interest, as if she'd never seen a human act so agitated before.

Beatrice—

Oh, no.

Thanks to Beatrice, I wasn't allowed anywhere near Hash Taggart. If I went over there to protect Noah and Hashtag and I got into a beef, that could be curtains for Beatrice—and definitely curtains for me when Brad found out. No way could I go there.

On the other hand, how could I not? It was my fault Noah was at Hardcastle Middle School. Sure, he got himself kicked out of the Academy. But if it hadn't been for me, he never would have managed it. If he got himself beaten to a pulp by Hashtag, in the end, it was on my head.

I couldn't let it happen. I headed for the door.

*Squeak!*

I looked down. The bowwow bone peeked out from under my sneaker. My eyes traveled to the slumbering Kandy. He was stirring. If he woke up, he'd head straight for his favorite toy. When he really got going with that thing, it could disturb the whole house. The last thing I needed was for Brad to search for me and find me on the one street I wasn't supposed to go to.

I carefully tweezered the bowwow bone between my thumb and forefinger and eased it silently into my pocket. Kandy rolled over and returned to sleep.

I tiptoed out the door and hit the sidewalk running. Staunton Street was at least a mile away, but I sprinted the full distance. Maybe I should have taken Brad up on a couple of those early-morning runs. My lungs were on fire when I rounded the corner, hoping against hope that I wasn't too late.

No—there he was, plodding up the sloping pavement, the weight of the chair under his arm bending him over to the right. Nussbaum wasn't kidding—those tight pants were practically spray-painted onto the skinniest legs in Hardcastle. From the bottom of the hill, he looked like a candy apple with an extra stick in it. Even among geniuses, Noah was special.

Struggling for breath, I rasped, "Noah!"

He turned, spied me, and hurried on. What a kid. He was determined to get himself massacred on my behalf.

Gasping for breath I no longer had, I pounded up the steep street. "Stop!" I tried to call, but it came out a pathetic wheeze. Forget it. I was going to have to physically tackle the kid on Hashtag's front walk.

Half dead, I overtook Noah from behind and clamped my arms around his puny shoulders. I had no wind left, so I just stood there, sucking air and holding on to him for dear life.

He had the nerve to pretend to be surprised to see me. "Hi, Donovan. I didn't know you got up this early."

There were a lot of things I could have said to that. But all I had breath for was "Go home!"

He tried to spin away, and his entire sweatshirt tore down the middle and wound up in my hands. All at once, I realized what his getup was supposed to be. The folding chair was the telltale sign. He was a WWE wrestler—bare chest, tights, and "boots." Except he didn't have much of a chest. He had ribs, though. You could count every last one of them.

This mental giant honestly believed that if he dressed like a wrestler, he could intimidate a guy like Hashtag. I would have laughed in his face, except for the fact that he was doing all this for *me*. In my family, I may have been lower in the pecking order than a deranged chow chow and her mongrel pup. But to this crazy kid, I was worth risking life and limb for. How could I yell at him? You know, if I had enough lung power left for yelling.

"Noah," I said gently, "if you take on Hashtag, you'll be a grease spot on the sidewalk."

He shook his head vehemently. "I've been training."

"Watching the Undertaker on YouTube isn't training!"

A tanker truck came laboring up the hill, gears grinding. I guided Noah back a few steps, and the truck made a wide three-point turn and reversed onto the sloped driveway just ahead of us. The logo on the tank read: OGDEN PROPANE DELIVERY.

In an obvious hurry, the driver jumped down from the cab and snaked a long hose around the side of the house, disappearing from view. A moment later, a mechanical pump began to hum.

Noah frowned. "That truck's not safely parked."

"Look who's thinking about safety all of a sudden," I retorted. "You're about to fight a grizzly bear—"

"I heard only partial application of the parking brake," Noah explained. "The slope of that driveway is at least twenty-seven degrees. Which means the weight of the tanker is exerting considerable force on the truck's transmission."

"Noah," I began warningly.

Noah didn't miss a beat. "Since it's early in the day, logic dictates that this must be one of the first deliveries. We therefore conclude the tank is mostly full. So, based on the average density of liquid propane—"

"Worry about the average density of Hashtag's fist," I interjected.

"—and assuming a tank capacity of six thousand US gallons, the maximum capability of the braking system should be exceeded just about"—he paused to calculate in his head—"now."

"Don't change the subject, Noah—"

There was a *snap*, and the truck lurched. With a crunch of tires, the big propane tanker began to roll forward down the steep driveway.

Uh-oh. "Mister!" I called around the side of the house. My breath had not fully returned, so I wasn't sure I could be heard over the sound of the pump. "Hey, mister!"

The tanker rolled out into the street, picking up speed. Heart sinking, I watched as the slope of the hill aimed it across the road toward a large Tudor-style home on the other side of Staunton.

"*Mister!*" Where was the driver? I could see the hose unrolling from its spool as the truck headed for the opposite curb. The guy had no idea of the disaster that was unfolding out here. When the tank smashed into that home . . .

There was no time to think. In a full-blown panic, I took off after the truck. I jumped up onto the running board right when the front tires bumped onto the lawn, heading straight for the house. I reached my arms in the open window and grabbed at the steering, tearing a dangling St. Christopher medal off the visor. I got both hands on the wheel and yanked in an attempt to avoid the building. The steering mechanism was locked. The truck continued on its path, rumbling down the grade of the lawn toward a large picture window set into a brick wall.

Desperately, I scanned the cab. The engine was set in park, which explained why the wheel wouldn't turn. I threw myself forward, got my hand on the gearshift, and yanked the control into N for neutral. My momentum sent me tumbling headfirst into the tanker, with my legs still flailing out the window. By the time I lifted my face out of the seat, the brick wall filled the windshield, coming up fast.

There was only one second to act and I did. I wrenched the wheel hard left. The truck responded instantly. It shaved the corner of the house, snapping off the passenger side mirror. It smashed through a wooden fence, roared across the backyard, and took a nosedive into a large swimming pool.

Amazed to be still alive, I struggled out of the

sinking cab, banging my head against the top of the window opening.

*Don't faint,* I told myself. *You'll drown.*

By the time I swam to the side and opened my stinging eyes, something large and metal was swinging at my nose. I ducked out of its way and resurfaced to see Noah holding the folding chair out over the water.

"Grab this and I'll rescue you!"

"I don't need rescuing," I shot back.

*"Grab it!"*

So I did. Instead of pulling me out, Noah toppled over the side into the pool beside me.

"I can't swim!" he burbled.

Why didn't I know that?

Treading water, I dragged him over to the side and hauled the two of us out onto the deck. We lay there for a second, panting. A huge bubble blurped from the cab of the truck as it sank to the bottom.

"You're a hero!" Noah told me in an awed tone.

"I can't be!" I hissed. "I'm not allowed to be here!"

"If it wasn't for you, the truck would have hit the house and exploded!"

I scrambled to my feet, pulling him up with me. "If I get caught on Hashtag's street, Beatrice is dead meat! No one can find out about this!"

"But, Donovan—"

"Promise you won't tell anyone!" I choked at him.

An anguished voice sounded in the distance. *"My truck!"* I could hear the driver's heavy footfalls as he pounded across Staunton Street.

I grabbed Noah, boosted him over the fence into the next yard, and clambered after him.

Noah looked down at my hand. "What's that?"

I checked. It was the St. Christopher medal from the truck, the broken chain still tangled around my fingers. I ripped it off and dropped it to the grass.

Noah picked it up. "It's a souvenir of your heroism!" he exclaimed.

"Stop saying that!" I peered through a knothole in the fence as the tanker driver burst into the backyard. When he took in the spectacle of his truck at the bottom of the pool, he let fly a series of words that would have sent my mother running for a sponge to wash his mouth out with soap.

The back door of the house slid open and four seriously agitated pajama–clad people ran out—a mother, father, and two kids. At the sight of the tanker in the pool, the boy, who looked about ten, dashed back inside, returned with a phone, and started snapping pictures. He had a slight limp that got worse when he ran.

"What happened here?" the dad demanded.

The driver was almost too upset to speak. "I thought the brake could handle it. But the slope was too steep. . . ." Unable to finish the explanation, he gestured around to the front and across the street, indicating the path his truck had taken.

The family stared at the deep tire tracks that crossed the lawn all the way to the pool deck.

"It's a miracle!" the mother breathed. "It could have destroyed our home, but it turned at the last minute."

"It was no miracle," the driver told her. "It was that kid!"

"What kid?" the father asked.

"I didn't get a good look at him," the driver admitted. "I only saw his feet."

"His feet?" the mom queried.

"He jumped into the cab and steered around your house with his feet sticking out the window. Like one of those Olympic swimmers cutting through the water—you know, a scissor-kick. Bravest, craziest thing in the world! He must be some kind of super-kid!"

"Superkid?" repeated the daughter.

I was just reflecting that she sounded kind of familiar when Noah took my spying place at the knothole and whispered, "It's Megan from cheerleading!"

"Shhh!" I hissed sternly. He was right! Megan Mercury—I'd forgotten she and Hashtag were neighbors. Of all the houses in town, I had to save the one belonging to the alpha bigmouth in school.

Megan's mom switched on the pool lights and everybody took a close look at the submerged truck. "Thank goodness there's nobody down there," she exclaimed after a moment. "This wonderful boy might very well have saved all our lives. It would be awful if it cost him his own!"

"But why would he leave after doing such an incredible thing?" the father mused. "He deserves to be honored for it."

"Is that a *chair*?" the son asked in amazement. "Was he sitting down when he saved us?"

"Don't be stupid," Megan snapped at him. "This is serious. We've got a real hero in our town. Don't you think it's important to find out who he is?"

Well, *I* didn't think it was important. On the contrary, nothing was more important than keeping the hero's identity a deep, dark secret. And when I heard police sirens in the distance, that became Job One. I grabbed Noah, and we snaked through backyards, climbing over fences and wrestling our way through hedges to put as much distance as possible between us and this act of heroism. We were soaked to the skin, scratched from head to toe, and covered in mud and grass when I left him at his front door.

"Remember—act natural," I told him, and then realized it was the most ridiculous thing I'd ever said. He was shivering and shirtless, his long underwear plastered to his skinny body and dripping what looked like black paint all around his dress shoes. There was definitely nothing natural about him.

He regarded me gravely. "Donovan, I'll never forget what I saw you do today."

I lost my temper. "You *have* to forget it, because it *never happened*!"

He reached under the waistband of his long johns and drew out the St. Christopher medal. "This will always be my most prized possession."

"Hide it!" I practically yelled. "Swear to me, Noah, that you'll never tell anybody that I was the guy who jumped into that truck and saved the Mercury house."

"But Donovan, people should know—"

*"Swear!"*

"All right, all right. I swear. I swear on the memory of Einstein, Max Planck, and Sir Isaac Newton."

And I had to be satisfied with that.

At home, I caught my first break of the entire morning. No one was up, and I was able to sneak back into my room unseen except by Beatrice. She lifted her fuzzy head from where she was sleeping next to Kandy and greeted me with a swish of her tail.

"The world almost ended today, kiddo," I told her, "but I think we got away with it."

Man, did I dream big.

# 8

# SUPERANONYMOUS
## MEGAN MERCURY

## MYSTERIOUS "SUPERKID"
## SAVES HOME, FAMILY

HARDCASTLE. It had all the elements of a Hollywood movie. A runaway truck filled with highly explosive propane. A darkened home and a sleeping family, completely unaware of the menace hurtling toward them. And a selfless young hero coming out of nowhere to risk life and limb to save the day, and just as suddenly disappearing into the shadows.

"He could have been killed, that kid," marveled Stanley Kaminsky, the driver of the propane truck. "That tanker hits the house—kaboom! You always hear about these crazy heroes who put their lives on the line to save a bunch of total strangers, but you never expect to see it in real life. This is no regular kid. He's more like a superkid!"

*Superkid.*

The word kept echoing in my head, usually in cheer form, since that was how my mind worked: *Two, four, six, eight, who do we appreciate? Superkid! Superkid! Go, Superkid!*

Or maybe a spell-it-out cheer: *Give me an S . . . Give me a U . . . !*

My family didn't have my cheerleader's positivity.

Mom was freaking out. "Our house was nearly destroyed—and us with it. We could have been killed. If that truck had exploded, who knows how big the fire would have been?"

My kid brother, Peter, was crazy enough to think the whole thing was a fabulous adventure. The town newspaper was paying him two hundred bucks for his pictures of the propane truck in our pool. When he saw "Photo by Peter Mercury" on the front page of the *Hardcastle Post*, he was running around the kitchen, punching the air and celebrating his newfound status as a celebrity.

My dad was the worst. He kept glancing out the front window, looking for the next propane truck with our name on it. He rarely made it through a single sentence without using some form of the word "sue." But what would have been the point of that? We were fine. The propane company was paying for the damage to the fence, the lawn, and the pool. Peter was even up two hundred bucks.

Talk about missing the point. Here was my family obsessing over an explosion that never happened, a lawsuit that would never be filed, and a photo credit in a dinky town newspaper that nobody ever read. And all the while, they were ignoring the most important part of this. Somewhere out there was an unsung hero who'd saved our house and maybe even our lives. This was *huge*!

And we didn't have the faintest idea who it was.

It was definitely a kid. According to Mr. Kaminsky, the driver, it was a boy around my age—middle school or maybe early high school. I thought of Hashtag right away, because he lived just up the block and was such a great athlete. But Hashtag slept till noon on non-game weekends, and besides, his arm was injured. Plus, Hashtag said it wasn't him.

The only other clue was the chair—a metal folding chair at the bottom of our pool. But there weren't any fingerprints on it, which may or may not have been because it had been underwater. The police had no explanation for how it might have gotten there.

At school, the buzz was all about the missing hero. Nothing ever happened in a boring town like Hardcastle, so a near disaster wasn't something that came along every day. Add to that the fact that the almost-victim was a popular head cheerleader—*Go me!*—and you had really big news. Throw a mystery into the mix, and nobody could even think about anything else.

"But surely *you* know who it is," Vanessa prompted me. "Didn't you see him running away or something?"

I shook my head. "The whole family was asleep. I heard a crash when it went through the fence and a splash when it hit the water. By the time we ran outside, there was no one around but the driver."

Zane Menash, one of the lacrosse players, was unimpressed. "As far as I'm concerned, the guy's an idiot. He's got a chance to be famous, get his name in the paper, maybe be on TV. Who knows? There might even be a reward. And what's he doing? Hiding like a scared rabbit."

"Maybe he thinks he'll get in trouble for putting the tanker in the pool," Hashtag suggested.

"Are you kidding?" I shot back. "Better in the pool than in the living room. There's no way this kid doesn't know what a great thing he did. You all saw what it said in that article in the *Post*."

I must have read it at least fifty times. At the bottom of the page, the very last paragraph went like this:

. . . Police are continuing to search for clues to the identity of this hero. He appears to have exited the scene by climbing over the fence into the neighbors' yard, but from there, the trail goes cold. If you're reading this, Superkid, it's time for you to step forward and reveal yourself. A grateful public wants to thank you for your bravery.

"Maybe he's just shy," Vanessa suggested.

"He wasn't too shy to jump into a speeding truck," Hashtag pointed out.

"Heroic instinct," I explained. "If you're a hero, you just are. It doesn't matter whether you're stopping a mugging or running into a burning building to save people." I had the most authority to talk about heroism since I was the only kid in school who'd been saved by an actual hero.

"So why the disappearing act?" Zane persisted.

"You guys don't get it," I told them. "He's modest. Some people don't have to be celebrated for every good deed. For a true superkid, just helping out is thanks enough." Why was it so hard for people to imagine a genuine Good Samaritan in our midst?

I must have had that conversation—or one just like it—ten times that day. Even the teachers were fascinated, thinking that this amazing hero might be someone they saw every day in one of their classes. Not to be negative, but middle schools were filled with a lot of dimwits who never thought beyond their next hot dog, video game, or shade of lip gloss. The idea that any one of us might turn out to be the superkid was pretty exciting for the faculty, too.

The only person who had no interest in the mystery was the guy who might as well have been from Mars. Yes, Noah was still on the cheerleading squad, sad to say. Ms. Torres was sticking to her decision not to let me kick him off. I was starting to think she was doing it on purpose—a test of my positivity. Believe me, any cheerleader who could smile through Noah's performances could smile through a killer tornado.

At practice that day, we were stretching and Noah was doing his regular whatever it was he did—a cross between knee bends and the death throes of a stick insect that's been run over by a bike. He heard us talking about the superkid and went even paler than usual.

"What's wrong, Noah?" asked Kelsey Leventhal.

His lips pinched together and turned dead white, and he ran for the boys' locker room like the police were after him.

"Wow," I commented, frowning. "If I'd known it was that easy to get rid of him, I would have had my house almost blow up weeks ago."

Some of the girls thought I was kidding.

# 9

# *SUPER*SECRET
## NOAH YOUKILIS

I never thought I'd see anything in real life as amazing as the stuff on YouTube.

This was logical. YouTube was the sum total of human experience. But since it was impossible to watch it all, viewers were naturally drawn to those videos that were the most exciting, entertaining, funny, or unusual. In other words, YouTube may have been life, but *our experience of YouTube* was the equivalent of life's greatest hits.

And then Donovan Curtis jumped into that truck and blew everything else away.

It won't ever be on YouTube, but it ran in my head on an endless loop, page views mounting—Donovan, sprinting, catching up to the rolling truck, heaving himself in the window; the tanker accelerating toward the house, disaster unavoidable; and then, at the last second . . .

I was getting crazy just thinking about it.

Donovan was famous for getting himself in trouble because he always acted without thinking. But here was proof that thinking was overrated. If he had taken time to think, the truck would have been out of reach, and Megan's house would have gone up in a fireball.

I'd studied the great heroes of humanity—people like Mahatma Gandhi, Nelson Mandela, and Dr. Martin Luther King Jr. But Donovan wasn't just someone I'd read about. He was my best friend. And I witnessed his act of great heroism with my own eyes. I even participated a little when I fell in the pool at the end and got really bad crotch chafing on the long wet walk home. This was living history!

But the more I thought about those heroes of the past, the more I realized that they'd had an advantage

Donovan didn't—they were free to tell their stories to the world. Donovan couldn't admit that he was the person they called superkid because then he'd have to explain what he was doing near Hashtag's house. That was technically my fault—*I* was the reason he'd been on Staunton Street. But how could I regret that? If Donovan hadn't come to intercept me, no one would have been there to protect the Mercurys.

The frustration of it was killing me. Donovan deserved so much credit. And how much was he going to get? Zero. I hadn't even been able to stand up to Hashtag for him. Now it was too late for that—I promised Donovan I'd stay away.

Just seeing him stressing over the whole situation broke my heart. He should have been having parades thrown in his honor, and getting the key to the city. Instead, he was hiding like a criminal, as if he'd done something terrible.

Every time someone talked about the superkid, his head would sink a little farther into his shoulders, like a neutron star collapsing into a black hole.

"Donovan, we have to tell everyone," I urged. "Whatever trouble you get in won't matter when people find out what a hero you are."

The things he threatened to do to me would have

been scary if they hadn't been anatomically impossible.

"Actually, there's no way to pull someone's liver out through his ear canal," I said gently. But I got the point, which was: *Never, never, never, never, never.*

Over the PA, when Principal Verlander was done with his usual announcements, he introduced head cheerleader Megan Mercury, who had something special to say. Her voice was like I'd never heard it before—emotional. Not that she didn't get emotional when she was yelling at me, but this was a different kind of emotion.

"Some of you know that a terrible thing almost happened to my house and my family this weekend," she announced. "But it didn't, thanks to a very brave person who might be listening right now. If you're out there, Superkid, please come forward and let us thank you properly."

While she was speaking, students stopped opening lockers and storing books and backpacks. They looked away from their phones and paid attention. You could have heard a pin drop in the hall. And when she was done, they all applauded—not wildly, but politely and with respect. By the time it was over, Donovan was bright red and you could see his carotid artery pulsing in his neck.

We had an assembly that morning. Our superintendent, Dr. Schultz, made another plea for the superkid to come forward.

"Now, I know you're a modest young man, and it might be embarrassing or uncomfortable to be made such a fuss of. But just as you were generous with your courage when you saved that house, we're asking you to be generous with yourself. Don't deprive your Hardcastle neighbors of a hero who can unite us all."

Walking out of that assembly, I felt so bad for Donovan, I could have wept.

I tried everything to console him. "Don't worry, Donovan. All these people—Schultz, the police, Megan—they're just fishing. I've analyzed the situation from every angle, and there's no way anybody but the two of us could find out that you're—you know—that guy."

In the thinning crowd exiting the cafeteria, those two boys named Daniel sauntered over to us.

"Hey, Donovan," called Daniel Nussbaum. "How was your weekend?"

"Do anything special?" added Daniel Sanderson.

"You know, apple picking, video games, clipping your toenails, saving a house from going up in a fireball . . . ?"

I was so shocked that I almost blacked out, but Donovan wasn't even surprised. "Shut up, you guys! I'm in big trouble if this gets around."

"But—but—but—" I stammered at both Daniels. "How could you know?"

"Oh, please," D. Nussbaum told me. "I saw you over on Staunton Street Saturday morning, dressed like a circus clown, so I called Donovan to keep you away from Hashtag. And, lo and behold, there's an almost-catastrophe on the same street at exactly that time. Who do we know who's crazy enough to jump onto a runaway propane tanker?"

"He wasn't being a hero," put in D. Sanderson. "He was just being Donovan."

That made me mad. "Donovan was so a hero! I mean"—I dropped my voice—"if he did the thing, which, of course, he didn't."

Donovan held his head. "I wish I'd never seen that propane truck."

"Nice talk," D. Nussbaum clucked. "Sure, a whole family might get barbecued, but Donovan's not in a heroic mood today—"

"*Obviously*, I don't regret saving the house," Donovan interrupted. "But now nobody's going to rest until they've found their superkid—not Megan, not her family, not the cops, not Schultz. I'm going to swipe Brad's fatigues and deploy back to Afghanistan in his place. I'll have to spend the rest of my life hiding out in his tank. That's the only place they won't look for me. How do I get myself into these messes?"

"Oh! Pick me!" D. Sanderson waved his hand. "Remember that time at the preschool book fair when you dumped all that superglue into the Clifford suit and Mr. Biaggio got stuck in it for three days?"

D. Nussbaum sighed. "Good times. Remember all the money we raised went to pay for a new Clifford suit because they had to cut a hole in the old one so he could go to the bathroom?"

"This is the same thing," D. Sanderson concluded. "You're older, but you aren't any smarter. And just like you were terrified that someone was going to notice that your fingers were glued together, now you're afraid that someone's going to find out you're the superkid."

"Don't say that word!" Donovan pleaded.

"What word?" D. Nussbaum asked innocently. "Oh, you mean *superkid*? Don't worry, you definitely won't hear me saying *superkid*."

And the two of them danced off down the hall, chanting, "*Superkid . . . superkid . . . superkid . . .*"

The bell rang, sending us to our next classes. I watched Donovan trudge away, slumped under the weight of his worry. He seemed to trust the two Daniels, even though I found it hard to, since they were doing the polar opposite of what they'd just promised. Maybe that was because the three of them had been friends since preschool. Maybe I was missing something.

No, that couldn't be it.

I owed so much to Donovan. If it hadn't been for him, remedial classes would be a distant dream for a guy like me. I'd still be in the gifted program, getting straight A's and hating them. He was the person who first showed me YouTube and opened my eyes to a whole world that couldn't be predicted by mathematical equations or scientific formulas—not even by me.

I had to find a way to help him.

# 10
# SUPERPHONY
## DONOVAN CURTIS

t was still dark out when Brad tapped on my bedroom door. "I'm heading out for a run," he informed me.

I rolled over and murmured something about catching all the details on CNN. Or maybe I just dreamed that part.

"Any chance you'll be joining me?"

He never gave up. Where was Beatrice? Asleep? It was her job to protect me from her owner before the sun came up. I tossed my pillow at her usual spot on the floor.

There was a canine squeal of outrage—an octave too high to be coming from Beatrice. I sat bolt upright just in time to see Kandy wriggling out from under the pillow bomb, yapping excitedly.

Brad barked a sharp command for silence, which might have worked if Kandy had been a Marine. The puppy upped the volume, circling the room like a mad dervish. That jarred Beatrice awake, and she added her howling to the chaos.

"Listen, Brad," I pleaded. "You can yell at Beatrice and me, but lay off Kandy! He's just a baby!"

From down the hall, a new cry joined the chorus— the other baby in our house, Tina.

Brad glared at me. "Way to go, Donnie."

"I haven't done anything!" I defended myself. "I was sleeping!"

"Do you ever listen to yourself?" Brad asked. "It's always 'I' and 'me.' But I know one kid in Hardcastle who isn't so self-centered. He always puts others first and himself second, and is willing to risk his life to do what's right."

My ears started to burn. I knew exactly where he was going with this.

In the five days since last Saturday, the mysterious hero who saved the Mercury home had gone from uplifting human-interest story to the town legend. You couldn't be anywhere in Hardcastle without overhearing that name on somebody's lips. From the school halls to the checkout line at the market to Channel 4 news, it was all superkid, all the time. Senior citizens discussed his great deed in cafes. Kindergartners played superkid in the park, sliding down slides, rescuing imaginary houses from imaginary disasters. Adults traded theories of who this star could be, and why he was choosing to keep his identity secret. Yesterday, I actually overheard a mom telling her two-year-old, "Eat your carrots and you'll grow up to be just like the superkid." It was like Batman lived in town. Better than Batman—there were people in Gotham City who didn't like him. *Everybody* loved the superkid.

It wasn't just Brad. Out of an entire superkid-obsessed community, my family turned out to be the biggest fans. Did it hurt that I couldn't reveal myself to them? You bet it did. What made it even harder to take was that they used him against me, holding him up as a shining example of everything I wasn't. I was selfish; the superkid thought only of others. I was whiny; the superkid never complained. I was afraid of a little exercise; the superkid put his life on the line.

Brad was constantly lecturing me: "A workout routine is a commitment to physical fitness. I'm sure the superkid would agree with that."

I knew for a fact that the superkid strongly disagreed. Honestly, I spent so much time biting my tongue that I'm amazed I didn't chew it off and choke on it.

For the next hour, I struggled to get Beatrice and Kandy settled while listening to Katie trying to calm Tina. Brad chimed in with updates: "All right, little girl, it's oh-five-thirty. Lights out, hit the sack . . ." Or, "Eyes shut, on your 'six,' pacifier deployed, diapers secure . . ."

I almost laughed at that one but swallowed the sound because Kandy had finally drifted off, sprawled out in his usual position. Seriously, the only thing missing was the chalk outline from the police department.

*Diapers secure.* Somehow, I doubted that appeared anywhere in the official Marine Corps training manual.

At last, the house was quiet again—except for me. I tossed and turned while everybody else slept. I got out of bed, padded down the hall to the bathroom, and flicked on the light.

Brad sat on the lid of the toilet seat, still in his

jogging clothes, snoring softly, holding his slumbering daughter against his chest. I rushed to turn the light off again, but it was too late. His tank commander's eyes—trained to be alert for any sudden danger—were open and on me.

He put a finger to his lips and whispered, "Just got her back down."

I nodded, thinking of Kandy. Baby humans and puppies weren't much different in that way. Once awake, they were ready for action.

Brad shot me a piercing gaze that made me grateful for Tina's presence. Without her, I'd be getting chewed out again.

But no—his expression wasn't angry. He seemed stressed and even . . . sad?

"Everything okay, Brad?" I asked in a low voice.

He replied, "I'm not good at this."

It was the last thing I expected to hear. Going by Brad, Marines were good at everything. It was part of what made them Marines. "What are you talking about? You got her back to sleep, didn't you?"

"Because she cried herself into exhaustion. Outstanding."

I shrugged. "Whatever gets the job done."

He heaved a sigh. "When I'm deployed, I always know

exactly what to do. In a potentially hostile situation, there are rules of engagement. If the tank breaks down, I'm ready for it. If the latrine backs up, there's a plan for that, too. But here—with my own family—I'm lost."

"I guess the real world isn't much like the military," I offered.

"The real world isn't military enough," he complained. "When you can take out a moving target thirty-five hundred meters away, do you know how it feels to look at your own daughter and not have the faintest idea what to do with her?"

I was blown away. Brad came across as the most confident, capable master of the universe you could ever meet. But here he was, almost human, just like the rest of us.

"Well, you could try baby talk," I suggested. "You know, goo-goo, ga-ga and stuff like that. It works for Katie."

He looked disapproving. "Verbal commands should be simple and concise, and convey exactly what you want to communicate in as few words as possible."

"But you're not communicating," I reminded him. "You're chilling. Baby style."

He actually seemed to consider my advice.

There was a first time for everything.

When I got to school later that morning, there was a bottleneck of kids at the main entrance. That was unusual. Unlike the Academy, the students of Hardcastle Middle weren't generally so eager to get educated that they'd line up for the privilege.

When I got close to the front, I could see what was going on, and it turned my blood to ice. There at the door stood three adults—Principal Verlander, Dr. Schultz, and Mr. Kaminsky, the driver of the tanker truck. They were looking into the faces of every boy as they entered the building. The purpose was clear—to give the one person who'd seen the superkid a chance to recognize him again.

My first impulse was to slip out of line and take off down the street. But if anybody saw me do it, I'd be putting extra suspicion on myself and then I'd get caught for sure. No, I had to brazen it through—walk right past the guy, head held high, and pray that he hadn't gotten a good look at me on Saturday.

As we shuffled forward, a familiar gnawing spread outward from my stomach until my entire body was vibrating with it. I'd spent so much of my life cowering in terror because I'd done something awful. Now I'd finally done something good—great even. And here I was, still cowering. Chloe would have called that irony. She got straight A's in English.

And then the driver's eyes were on me. My breath caught in my throat. My heart skipped a couple of beats. But then the eyes shifted to the kid behind me. Zero recognition—hooray! I practically collapsed into the school, bowled over with relief. I'd made it.

My relief lasted less than the distance to my locker. A sharp burst of laughter made me jump.

"Dude, you look terrible!" Nussbaum exclaimed. "What is this—Zombie Day?"

"That would explain the mystery meat in my sausage biscuit from the cafeteria," Sanderson added.

"I'm thrilled my sleep deprivation is giving you so much enjoyment," I said sarcastically. "There's a newborn baby at my house. It isn't all Pampers and peekaboo, you know. That kid's got a set of lungs like an air raid siren." I told them about my morning—Brad waking me, me waking Kandy, Kandy waking Beatrice, and the two of them waking Tina.

They had a nice long laugh at my expense. Having friends was a wonderful thing. No wonder Noah was so gung ho about it.

And speaking of Noah . . .

"Have you guys seen Noah today?"

Sanderson shook his head. "I think he might be absent."

"I doubt it," I said. "He loves regular school so much that he doesn't want to miss a second of it. He's usually the first one here and the last to go home." That was another reason Noah was totally unique in the history of Hardcastle Middle.

"Maybe his perfect attendance record is spoiling his shot at remedial classes," Nussbaum suggested.

"Well, if you see him, let him know I'm looking for him."

They gave me a hard time about that, too, but it didn't matter because Noah really was absent. The other big news was that Mr. Kaminsky didn't recognize anyone else as the superkid. That came as no surprise to me. So there was no wild celebration in the building—not unless you count Megan Mercury's reaction when she realized Noah wouldn't be at cheerleading practice.

When I got home, the door was locked, and I had to pound on it for close to five minutes before anybody let me in.

"Sorry, Donnie!" Mom tossed over her shoulder as

she dashed into the living room. "We're all watching TV."

"What's on?" I asked without much interest.

"Breaking news!" she enthused. "They found the superkid!"

So help me, I actually turned around in the foyer, half expecting to see a news crew with TV cameras pointed at me.

"So when you say they 'found' him," I ventured cautiously, "you mean they know who he is, and they're about to announce the name . . . ?"

"Get in here, Donnie!" Mom was practically giddy. "You don't want to miss this."

I sure didn't. I rushed into the living room. Mom, Katie, and Brad were on the edge of their seats, staring with bated breath at the screen, which showed the empty briefing room at Hardcastle City Hall. Even Tina, in Katie's arms, seemed riveted to the TV, although nothing was going on. Ditto Beatrice, who seemed to pick up on the supercharged expectation that something huge was about to happen.

Only Kandy was immune. According to Mom, the puppy was inconsolable every minute I was at school— like he thought I was gone for good or something.

Overjoyed at my return, he made his usual bull run at me, tripping over his huge feet, and rolling into a skull-rattling collision with my ankle. He finally came to a stop with all four legs clamped around my jeans. I shook him off before he could make a liquid deposit on my shoes.

Everyone was frozen in anticipation, nobody more than me. So the driver had recognized me after all. Why didn't they just talk to me on the spot? Why ignore me then and wait seven hours to announce my name on TV to the whole town? Was this supposed to be a happy surprise for me, a reward for my heroics?

My dad burst in the front door and hustled past me into the living room. "What's going on? Did it happen yet?" He almost never came home from work in the middle of the day.

Mom pointed to the screen. "Here comes the mayor. I can't remember the last time I was this excited."

Mayor DaSilva was beaming as he assumed the podium. "I know I speak for every citizen of Hardcastle when I say that we've all walked a little taller and felt a lot of pride since learning about an impressive young hero in our community. At long last, this remarkable teenager has stepped forward to receive our appreciation and gratitude. Superkid, come on out here and receive the applause of a grateful city."

Wait—the kid was *there*? How was that possible? I was *here*!

My relief was dwarfed by my bewilderment. This "hero" was a phony! Why would some random guy come forward to try to take credit for what *I* did? What was his angle?

Obviously, he was looking for fame and glory—and maybe some reward money. But wasn't that risky, knowing the real superkid was out there somewhere? I mean, I couldn't come forward—but *he* didn't know that. He could go from hero to goat in the blink of an eye. Plus, he could get in serious trouble if he accepted a cash reward. You'd have to be really stupid to take a gamble like that.

The imposter appeared in a doorway and took his place onstage beside the mayor. There he stood, basking in the cheers and the camera flashes.

I nearly dropped dead right there in my own living room.

"Hey, Donnie," Dad piped up, "isn't that your little friend from genius school?"

I couldn't answer.

Noah Youkilis.

Mom fixed me with an accusing stare. "Why didn't you say anything?"

"This is—news to me too," I managed to stammer.

Noah! What was he trying to pull? Did he think people would just take his word for it that he'd leaped into a moving truck? He couldn't run—not without kicking himself in the butt with his flailing heels. Man, he couldn't cross a schoolyard hopscotch court without tripping over the number five. Anyone who'd ever seen his cheerleading routines would know that! Why would he expect anybody to believe him?

He reached into his pocket and pulled out a silver necklace on a broken chain. The TV cameras zoomed in on it. It looked kind of familiar, but I couldn't quite place where I'd seen it before.

"What have you got there, son?" asked Mayor DaSilva.

Noah looked nervous as he shifted his praying-mantis posture. "This is the St. Christopher medal that was hanging from the visor in the propane tanker," he explained, a little stiffly. "It snapped off in my hand when I jumped in through the window and grabbed for the steering wheel . . ."

Oh, no.

I'd totally forgotten the St. Christopher medal! Why, oh why did I let him keep it? He said he just wanted it for a souvenir! How was I supposed to know he'd use it as Exhibit A to prove he was something he wasn't?

Why was he doing this? So he could be a celebrity? He was *already* a celebrity at the Academy! He could have been a titan just by doing his homework and not working against his own natural abilities!

Noah went on to describe the events of last Saturday morning. He knew every detail because he'd been there, watching me. And of course, he added all this extra science info like the density of liquid propane, the acceleration of a truck down a driveway pitched at twenty-seven degrees, and blah, blah, blah. He sounded nerdy but also authoritative. Then the mayor took over again and said that in addition to being this great hero, Noah was also the owner of the highest IQ in the history of Hardcastle.

My brother-in-law shook his head in disbelief. "I knew he was smart, but I never dreamed he had guts like that. You could learn a thing or two from him, Donnie."

"I learn new things from him every day," I said through clenched teeth.

"See, Tina?" Katie cooed to the baby in her arms.

"That's your Uncle Noah. He's a hero."

Tina gurgled and spit up a little.

I wracked my brain but couldn't remember my sister telling her daughter anything good about her Uncle Donovan.

"Next time he comes over," Brad decided, "I'll talk to him about a career in the Marine Corps."

Oh, perfect. Noah, whose lack of physical control sent one of his fellow cheerleaders to the emergency room, would be great behind the controls of an M1 tank.

The press conference ended to tremendous applause, a lot of it in my own living room. I had to admit that it bugged me. Not just that Noah was taking credit for something I did. After all, it wasn't as if I could take credit for it myself. But how could my family be so quick to believe all this? They *knew* Noah!

Worse, it was like they were comparing him to me. It went without saying that I wasn't as smart as Noah. But now I wasn't as bold, gutsy, and decisive either. Ditto noble, gallant, and self-sacrificing. And his ability to make things happen? I couldn't even come close.

Katie said, "I can't believe I never saw that in Noah before. He always seemed so . . ." She searched for the right word.

"Dweeby?" I suggested, annoyed. I had others—lying, double-crossing, shifty, back-stabbing . . .

"Cerebral," she concluded.

"Inner strength, that's what it is," Brad chimed in. "A hidden reservoir he can tap when things are really desperate."

Mom said, "Such a wonderful boy. What's wrong with you, Donnie? How come it's been so long since he's been over?"

"Noah's pretty busy these days," I explained. "He joined the cheerleading squad."

"Seriously?" Brad echoed, struggling to fit cheerleading into the role he pictured for Noah in his beloved Corps. Pom-poms clashed with dress blues.

"Relax," I soothed him. "Noah might be the worst cheerleader in the history of the world. He won't be shaking his booty for the Dallas Cowboys anytime soon."

"I'm sure Noah is *just fine*," Mom said pointedly. She turned to my sister. "Katie, you were a cheerleader in high school. I'll bet you could give Noah some pointers."

Katie nodded enthusiastically. "I used to really bring it back then."

"If you can teach that guy how to cheerlead, " I told her, "then we won't have one superkid. We'll have two."

"That's unkind," my mother clucked disapprovingly. "Set it up, Donnie. It would be nice for all of us to express to Noah how much we appreciate what he's done for the town."

"And it'll give Tina a chance to spend some time with her favorite uncle," Katie added.

I took that personally.

My father shook his head. Could it be? Someone finally coming to my defense?

He announced, "I just can't believe that the superkid would be friends with a guy like *you!*"

I called Noah all afternoon and well into the night. Again and again, his voicemail came up: *"I'm unable to take your call for any one of hundreds of thousands of possible reasons predicted by chaos theory. So leave a message at the beep."*

"It's Donovan," I snapped after the tone. "Call me."

He never did.

I gave up on the phone and went over to the Youki-lis house. The place was jumping. When I got there,

Noah was taking a call from our state senator. I actually had to wait behind the owner of Hardcastle Lanes. He'd been there for an hour, he said, waiting to have his picture taken handing Noah a giant coupon awarding the entire Youkilis family free bowling for life. According to Noah's dad, it had been going on all day—local businesspeople lining up for a photo op shaking hands with the superkid.

Eventually, I snuck in the back door and cornered Noah when he was on his way to the bathroom. He seemed genuinely thrilled to see me. "Hi, Donovan. Guess what?"

"I don't have to guess what!" I hissed. "I know what. The whole town knows. What I *don't* know is *why would you do such a thing?*"

He seemed mystified. "I did it for you."

"For *me*? How do you figure that?"

"You were so scared that someone might figure out it was you," he explained. "Logic dictates that no one will look for the superkid if the superkid has already been found. And now you're safe."

I was honestly and truly speechless. I'd heard a lot of brilliance from Noah, and a lot of stupidity too. This seemed to be both at the same time.

"You're welcome," he added sincerely.

"Yeah—uh, great. Thanks," I stammered. "It's just that—well, what if nobody believes you?"

No sooner were the words out of my mouth than I realized what an idiotic question that was. Everyone believed him already. How else could you explain the lineup downstairs, the press conference with the mayor, and the love-fest in my living room?

"Why wouldn't they believe me?" he asked.

Where would you even start? From the vaulting horse he had to be thrown over to his performance as a cheerleader, there was no bigger klutz than Noah. And klutzes couldn't dive in through the windows of moving trucks. Didn't he think that sooner or later, someone would connect the dots?

Then again, this was the guy who believed you could learn to be a wrestler from YouTube, so maybe I had my answer.

He went on. "I have the driver's St. Christopher medal. I was there, so if anyone asks questions, I know exactly what happened. I fell in the pool too, so my parents can confirm that I was wet when I came home that morning. It's foolproof."

I looked him up and down, tracing the arc of his praying-mantis posture. "Well, that kind of depends on your definition of *fool*."

"And now you don't have to worry about being caught in Hashtag's neighborhood," he finished. "It's the least I can do after all the help and support you've given me since we met."

He was 1000 percent serious—and 1000 percent convinced he was doing me a great favor. It was a ridiculous sham, but what choice did I have other than to go along with it? Noah getting found out meant *me* getting found out. And since the whole story was so huge now, that would put ten times the attention on Beatrice being a dangerous animal.

I was stuck with it. My only hope was to coach Noah into acting like the hero he was supposed to be. We were partners in the biggest lie since I'd pretended to be in the gifted program.

Somebody once said, "The truth will set you free."

That was so wrong. All it could do was sink us.

# 11

## SUPERGRATEFUL
### MEGAN MERCURY

**W**ho knew?

Of all the people I thought might have turned out to be the superkid, Noah Youkilis was dead last on the list. This went far beyond not judging a book by its cover. You couldn't judge *this* book by its cover, pages, about-the-author section, or even the bar code and ISBN number on the back. There was nothing good about this book—not even if the store put it on special sale where they paid you to take it off their hands.

But there was no denying it. Noah had saved our lives and our home. He may have been the worst cheerleader in the history of humanity, but I owed him . . . everything.

*Two, four, six, eight, who do we . . .*

Even in my head, I couldn't force myself to finish the line.

*Appreciate! Appreciate! What's your problem, Megan? No sentence is more familiar to a cheerleader!*

But the appreciating wasn't the issue. It was the person getting appreciated.

When we went over to Noah's house to thank him in person, I tried to work up some of the emotions that I should have felt for him—gratitude, admiration, friendship. But one look at him and it just wasn't there. He was still the clumsy oaf who had single-handedly ruined my cheerleading squad. I strained to notice something positive about him that I hadn't seen before. Maybe his shoulders were broader than I remembered (they weren't). Or his voice was deeper (it wasn't). Or he was taller (oh, please) or more clear-eyed (he had conjunctivitis from severe seasonal allergies). Face it, if he'd kept the *Hindenburg* from exploding instead of one little propane truck, he'd still be Noah.

Mom, Dad, and Peter took turns hugging him, so I had to do it too. It was awful.

I told Noah, "I'm very grateful," because at least that part was true.

He said, "I'm glad it was your house." I know he meant it in a good way, but it made me want to punch him.

*Positivity,* I reminded myself.

I thought everything would be less painful once we were back at school, but that turned out to be wishful thinking. Principal Verlander called an assembly so we could all congratulate the superkid, and I had to hug him again—this time in front of nine hundred people. In the crowd, Ms. Torres kept gesturing at me, pointing to the sides of her mouth. That was the signal for more smiling, but I just couldn't pull it off. I was a cheerleader, not a wizard.

Wherever Noah walked in the halls, a buzz of excited conversation followed.

"That's him!"

"That's the superkid!"

"He saved Megan Mercury's life, you know!"

I got so sick of hearing it that I snapped. "He didn't save my *life*; he saved my *house*!" I hissed at the bewildered seventh grader. "And for all we know, the propane might not even have exploded!"

"Yeah, but if it had, then your house would have been on fire," he mused. "And maybe you wouldn't have gotten out alive."

"I would have made it," I insisted.

I thought I was keeping my voice low, but I guess I was too emotional. We were the center of attention. Worst of all, Noah himself was there, listening with keen interest.

"Oh, hi, Noah," I said, my face twisting. "We were just talking about what a great thing you did."

At lunch, I emerged from the food line to find my usual table completely full. All my friends and fellow cheerleaders were gathered around Noah—even Vanessa, who still had a bandage across the bridge of her nose. Noah was recounting the story with the propane truck, and they were hanging on his every word, worshipping the boy wonder.

"Weren't you scared?" asked Vanessa in a somewhat nasal tone.

"There wasn't time to be," Noah replied. "Protecting Megan's house was all that mattered. Of course, I didn't know it was Megan's house then. I just saw people in danger and realized *I* was the only one who could help them . . ."

I stood there balancing my tray and clearing my throat meaningfully. Nobody so much as glanced in my direction except Noah himself. He looked up and said, "Everybody move over and make room for Megan."

Suddenly, the idea of having to thank Noah *again* became just too much for me. "That's okay," I told him stiffly. "I've got a lot of homework to do before sixth period."

I selected a table on the opposite side of the cafeteria and sat down to eat. Every bite tasted like cardboard.

"Wow!" came a voice. "Megan Mercury's all alone in the lunchroom!"

I groaned. Daniel Nussbaum, my *second* favorite person in the whole school. There he was, with his best friend Daniel Sanderson—Tweedledum and Tweedledumber.

"Hey!" Sanderson exclaimed. "If we eat lunch with the head cheerleader, do you think we can become as cool as she is?"

"We'll never be as cool as the superkid," Nussbaum admitted. "But maybe we can make it up to Megan's level."

I glared at them. "Fine. Bust my chops. Get it over with quick so we can all eat in peace."

Sanderson slid across the bench next to me and took

a mighty bite of his egg salad sandwich. "You seem kind of cranky for someone who's just been saved from the jaws of death."

I didn't answer. These creeps were like a black hole that sucked up all my positivity. Maybe if I ignored them, they'd go away.

"Hey, guys, is that Noah sitting in the middle of all those cheer—"

It was Donovan Curtis. The minute his eyes fell on me, the word "cheerleader" died on his tongue.

"Noah's so popular now," Nussbaum exclaimed. "Who would have thought *he'd* turn out to be the superkid, instead of, you know, somebody else?"

"He never struck me as the stop-a-runaway-truck type," Sanderson agreed.

"It just shows how wrong you can be about a guy," Donovan replied, his words clipped.

I felt like they were saying one thing and meaning another. I could have asked about it, but that would have meant that I cared what these three idiots had to say. And believe me, I didn't.

"Noah *deserves* all the attention he's getting." So help me, they were making me crazy to the point where I was actually saying nice things about Noah. "Good for him."

"I guess Noah's going to be the guest of honor at your big birthday pool party this year," Nussbaum prodded, "seeing as how you're so grateful to him."

I dropped my fork. In all the excitement of the near disaster, I'd totally forgotten my party was coming up in a couple of weeks. How could I get away with not inviting the guy who'd made it possible for me to have another birthday in the first place?

"Well—" I stammered, "the—uh—invitations have already gone out—"

"Mine must have gotten lost in the mail," Sanderson concluded.

"—and the guest list is already set," I rambled on. Ever since elementary school, my annual birthday party had been the ultimate bash for kids in our grade. It was always the first pool party, right when the weather was starting to warm up. Best of all, I only invited cheerleaders, athletes, and the other cool people—which explained why Tweedledum, Tweedledumber, and TweedleDonovan never made the cut. And if the encyclopedia had a heading under *Least Likely to Be Invited*, there'd be a picture of Noah at the top of the page. It wasn't as if I'd decided not to invite him. It just never would have even crossed my mind for the billionth of a second that it would have taken to say no way.

But now . . .

"Of course Noah's on there," Nussbaum announced. "Can you imagine the kind of jerk Megan would look like if she didn't invite the guy who saved her life?"

"I might not have died!" I blurted. Then I covered up by adding, "And obviously Noah's invited. How shallow do you think I am?"

My appetite gone, I dumped my tray into the garbage and marched over to my usual table, where the superkid was still holding court.

"Hey, Noah," I called, "you're coming to my birthday party, right?" And I stormed out of the cafeteria without waiting to hear his answer.

Maybe his family would be out of town that weekend. A girl could dream.

It had been a lousy day, but at least I had a lacrosse game to look forward to that afternoon—at home against Rutherford Junior High. And when Noah didn't show up at the field house before the start, my heart soared. Could it be that the superkid was too important and too busy to be a cheerleader anymore? Maybe he had interviews to do, or calls of congratulations from the president and the queen of England. Maybe he was being measured for his wax figure at

Madame Tussauds. I didn't care, so long as it kept him away from my squad.

Rutherford were our neighbors and division rivals, and that always attracted a lot of students from both schools. The stands were full and the atmosphere was rowdy. I was balanced at the top of our human pyramid, when all at once, the crowd noise swelled to a roar. Everyone—even the Rutherford kids—were stomping on the metal bleachers and screaming. I threw my arms up in a gesture of triumph, but nobody was watching me. Nobody was watching any of the Lady Hornets, even though we trained as hard as the athletes and had made it to the middle school state cheerleading finals two years running.

From my vantage point at the apex, I saw what all the fuss was about. *He* had arrived. He jogged out onto the field in his clumsy, butt-battering style.

I screamed, "Abandon pyramid! Let me down!" because Noah was heading right for us, and for sure, he would take out the formation and send us all flying.

My dismount wasn't graceful, but at least I landed on my feet and not my head.

He blundered into our midst and the girls crowded around, high-fiving him. The audience went nuts, and it was pretty obvious that this was more than the usual ovation that he always got for falling flat on his face.

A chant rose from the stands: "*Su-per-kid! . . . Super-kid! . . .*"

My cheeks burned hot. I'd put my heart and soul into creating the greatest cheers and the best routines in the whole county, but all anybody wanted to look at was the guy with two left feet.

Noah was pushing his way through the squad toward me, shouting something that I couldn't hear over the crowd noise.

"What?" I demanded.

"Yes!" he replied.

"Yes, what? What are you talking about?"

"Yes, I'm coming to your party!"

All at once, the crush of people on our sideline parted and Hashtag stepped out in front of us. I was stoked. If there was one kid who appreciated Noah even less than I did, it was Hashtag, whose arm was still in a sling, thanks to a brouhaha Noah had been mixed up in. If anyone could knock the superkid down a peg, it had to be the town's top athlete.

The crowd grew quiet as the two of them confronted each other. Suddenly, Hashtag broke into a grin. With his free hand, he grasped Noah's wrist and raised his arm above his head, championship-boxer style. Fans of both teams went absolutely berserk.

I pulled Hashtag aside while Noah soaked up the glory. "Are you crazy? Why would you treat him like a hero in front of everybody?"

He actually seemed surprised by the question. "Because he *is* a hero. You know that better than anybody. You're the one he saved."

"*Might have* saved," I amended.

"Don't you think it's kind of cool? It's like going to school with Batman or something."

I glowered at him. "You're messing with me, right? Please tell me you've got the brains to tell the difference between *that guy* and Batman."

He shrugged. "Well, obviously Noah hasn't got real superpowers or anything like that. But how many of us ever get to meet a hero?"

I made a face. "So what? Hero or not, he's still a weirdo."

"I don't think that anymore," he informed me. "Shrimpy little kid like Noah—I should have been able to wrap him around my little finger. You know why I couldn't? Because he's the superkid. He hadn't saved anyone yet, but that was always inside him."

Look who'd turned into the big philosopher—

Hashtag, who half the time communicated via a series of grunts and scratched himself in his parents' picture window.

It was the perfect end to a perfect day.

At least we had something to cheer about. The Hornets destroyed Rutherford 9–1, even though Hashtag couldn't play. The team dedicated their first win to Noah, because he was their inspiration today. Hashtag himself handed Noah a game ball, signed by all the players.

Zane told him, "Every time I started to get tired, I thought: 'Where would we be if the superkid gave up? Where would Megan be?'"

Noah himself supplied the answer. "Burned up in the fire!"

"I might have escaped!" I yelled once again.

"No way," said Hashtag. "You would have been a goner."

Noah added, "He means considering the combustion temperature of propane and the wood framing underneath the brick of your home."

I wanted to hug him again—this time until he stopped breathing.

Rah, rah.

## 12
# SUPERSPOTTY
## CHLOE GARFINKLE

*<< Hypothesis: The greatest heroism can come from the last place you'd ever think to look for it. >>*

O r maybe it wasn't a real hypothesis, since it had already been proven right here in Hardcastle.

Noah Youkilis had thrown himself into a runaway truck and steered it away from a fiery collision with the house in its path. No one could talk of anything else. It was the kind of amazing story that happened in some other town, but not yours.

Even more amazing, the superkid who performed this miracle was one of *us*! Sure, the gifted students won spelling bees and science fairs and summer internships—that happened all the time. But here was proof that we could be more than good grades and high test scores. We weren't just the kids you'd go to when you needed homework help or someone to get that nasty virus off your laptop. We could make a *difference*. We could be *heroes*.

The best part was that it was *Noah*. The superkid turned out to be the super*gifted* kid. And exactly the strengths that *made* him gifted—a nimble mind, an understanding of science, an ability to analyze a variety of factors and instantly decide on a course of action—had saved the day. Those strengths were *our* strengths. He might have been the hero, but his triumph counted for all of us. You bet we were proud of him!

Of course, Noah didn't attend the Academy anymore, even though he was smarter than all of us put together. But he'd been on the gifted track with us most of the way. And he still came three afternoons a week for robotics—him and Donovan. No question he was *ours*. So when we heard the news, it was a big deal. We celebrated like it was someone from our own class.

We planned a little reception for him in the robotics lab on his first visit after the announcement. We hung streamers from the multicolored wires suspended like cobwebs from the ceiling, and we programmed our robot, Heavy Metal, to cross the room, stop in front of Noah, and raise a sign that read: CONGRATULATIONS, SUPERKID.

Everyone started peppering Noah with questions about his heroic moment. Noah responded in a very Noah-esque way—a lot about the properties of propane, the effects of gravity versus inertia on a vehicle stopped on a slope, and Archimedes's principles of buoyancy as applied to a tanker truck in a swimming pool. You know, easy stuff we'd all understood since elementary school.

"Okay, people, I've got a surprise for you," Oz announced. "Noah did an interview with *The Russ Trussman Hour* yesterday, and it's broadcasting in about two minutes. Take a seat, everybody. Let's watch our star in action."

We scrambled to our desks and the teacher turned on the flat screen at the front of the lab. Russ Trussman ran an interview show that had been on the air since our parents were our age. It was proof that Noah's story was spreading beyond just Hardcastle. *The Russ Trussman Hour* was out of the network affiliate a few towns over, and around here it was huge. Everybody watched Russ Trussman—all the adults, anyway.

We applauded the sight of Noah sitting on the couch that had hosted so many movie stars, sports heroes, and presidential candidates. And there in the host's chair was Trussman himself, the perfect teeth and the perfect tan, the store-bought nose, the perfect hair (also probably store-bought.).

*<< Hypothesis: The more famous you are, the fewer original body parts you have. >>*

"I can't believe Noah is on *Russ Trussman!*" exclaimed Jacey, who was normally the quietest kid in the Academy. No one was immune to Superkid-Mania.

The host asked Noah pretty much the same questions we had, and got pretty much the same answers. Noah seemed a little stiffer than usual but on the whole was fairly poised. After all, it had to be nerve-racking to have TV cameras pointed at you. The studio audience cheered every single statement he made, even when he answered "How old are you?" with "Thirteen years, two months, eleven days, six hours, and two-point-seven minutes—subject to Einstein's theory of general relativity, of course." Or maybe they thought he was kidding.

The screen showed video of an enormous crane winching the propane truck out of the Mercurys' pool while Noah recited the formula for determining how much lifting power was required. Surprisingly, the pool was undamaged, and was ready for use as soon as the fence around it could be repaired.

"How do you think that folding chair got into the water with the truck?" Trussman asked him.

Noah looked startled. "Folding chair?"

Trussman frowned. "Didn't you see it? It was the only other thing in the pool besides the tanker."

"I—I—maybe it's the Mercurys'."

"No, I asked them," Trussman replied. "They have absolutely no idea where it came from."

"Well, neither do I," Noah told him.

The host looked into the camera. "It seems we have a mystery on our hands. If any of our viewers can cast some light on where the mysterious chair came from, please call us at the studio. In a moment, we'll ask our superkid about his sky-high IQ and whether his superior intelligence helped him make the split-second decision that saved a home and probably the four lives inside it . . ."

As we watched the rest of the interview, I was distracted by the peculiar look on Noah's face when Trussman asked about the chair. It set off bells inside my head. Not the chair itself—I had no explanation for that. But the whole story sounded . . . It was hard to say, but . . .

What it *didn't* sound like was Noah.

How could that be, though?

<< *Hypothesis: Sometimes a gut feeling carries more weight than the so-called facts.* >>

Not that Noah wasn't a good person. Of course he'd want to help a family in danger. He might even try. But by the time he'd be done analyzing the situation, the fire from the explosion would have burned the house to the ground.

I tried to shake the thought out of my head. Why was I obsessing over this? Finally, the hero was one of us!

I needed him to be real.

But the more I thought about it, the more convinced I became that the Noah I knew could never have done what he was now so famous for doing.

When the interview ended we all applauded, even me. But my mind was whirling. The whole thing didn't make sense. And as a scientist, I wasn't a fan of things that didn't make sense.

Oz turned off the TV. "Congratulations, Noah. You were terrific. Now let's get some work done. Heavy Metal's pretty smart, but he's not going to program his own software."

As the rest of the team gathered around the robot, Donovan and I brought up the rear. I watched as Noah tripped over a cable, and only Oz's steady hand kept him from face-planting on the floor.

I grabbed Donovan's wrist. "It wasn't him," I whispered.

"Huh?"

"The superkid. It couldn't have been Noah."

"But"—it genuinely seemed to throw him—"but everybody says it was him. The mayor. The police chief. Even Russ Trussman!"

"I get that," I told him, "but it's just not possible. Listen, I love Noah—I'd never put him down."

"It's not that—" Looking miserable, Donovan glanced away from me to the opposite corner of the room, and murmured, "You have to promise not to tell anyone."

That brought me up short. "What? What are you talking about?"

He leaned in and whispered, "It was me."

"What was you?"

What he told me shocked me down to my toes—that *he*, not Noah, was the superkid. That he'd only been in the neighborhood to keep Noah from tangling with a bully named Hashtag (what kind of name was Hashtag?). And by some colossal illogic, I couldn't tell anyone about this because it would result in Beatrice being impounded by Animal Control and declared vicious. The more details he filled in, the nuttier it became.

I glared at him. "Where do you get off making up a story like that?"

"But it's true!" he pleaded.

"I sort of accept it from Noah, because he's—well, Noah. But you? I thought we were friends!"

"Look," he reasoned. "You figured out it couldn't be Noah. But it had to be somebody, right?"

"Not necessarily," I pointed out. "Maybe the truck changed direction when it thumped over the curb, so it missed the house and went into the pool. The simplest explanation for something is usually the correct one."

"The driver saw my legs sticking out the window!" he hissed in protest.

"Eyewitnesses can be undependable," I retorted. "When the tanker swerved, the driver assumed someone must have done it, and his mind filled in the rest. You two ought to be ashamed of yourselves. Did you and Noah cook this up to help him make a splash at Hardcastle?"

"Of course not," he countered. "If Noah wanted to be special, all he'd have to do is take an IQ test. The last thing he's looking to do is stand out."

At that moment, Noah announced, "Our lacrosse team is on a winning streak because of me. I hope I can have the same effect on robotics."

I shot Donovan a grimace and joined the others around Heavy Metal. Hey, I admired Donovan a lot. I'd been the first in the gifted program to appreciate what he had to offer. But what had made him so unique at the Academy was that he brought in an outside point of view that none of the rest of us had. He wasn't gifted—he was just normal.

Noah, on the other hand, was the opposite of normal. I'd worried what would happen to him in regular school, and now my worst fears were coming true. Once outside the academic atmosphere of the gifted program, he'd started craving the thrill of *popularity*, and Donovan had cooked up this cockamamie scheme to give it to him.

Well, maybe Donovan thought he was doing Noah a favor, but this could only end one way—with the superkid exposed as a fraud.

Why was I so surprised? Donovan's time in the Academy had been spent this way—always scrambling, a half step ahead of disaster.

<< *Hypothesis: A leopard never changes its spots.* >>

But this time he was taking poor Noah along for the ride.

# 13

## SUPERBLACKMAIL
### DANIEL SANDERSON
### & DANIEL NUSSBAUM

One thing about being friends with Donovan: It was never boring.

For us, boring was the enemy, and it had the edge over us. Boring was school's trademark. And school owned us a hundred and eighty days a year.

Donovan was our secret weapon against boredom. Like the time he opened the top of his uncle's convertible halfway through the carwash, or the zoo trip when he tried to see if a human could beat a chimpanzee at a poop-throwing contest. (The human lost.)

Sometimes we were there for the event itself. Others we just saw the aftermath, or rode with Donovan to the emergency room. We missed it when he tried to adopt the raccoon that had moved into the school's dumpster, but we got to go to the doctor's appointments for the rabies shots. Judging by the hollering, it was pretty painful. We could hear it from the waiting room. Sanderson recorded it on his phone, and we play it every now and then, when things get dull.

But of all the crazy stuff Donovan had done to keep boring away, this superkid business might have been his crowning achievement, because it tossed Noah into the mix. You didn't meet a lot of people who were a genius and an idiot at the same time. Noah was so smart that he moved the needle all the way around the dial back to stupid. Either that or his mind was far too brilliant to deal with ordinary dumb stuff like life.

Donovan couldn't admit he was the superkid. He needed a stand-in to cover for him. Noah.

It was the kind of mess that only happened to Donovan. And it really made it worth our while to go to school every day.

It was hard to get Noah alone lately. He was always

surrounded by admirers. After all, Superman had Clark Kent; Batman had Bruce Wayne; Spider-Man had Peter Parker. But Noah had no secret identity to hide behind. Everybody knew who the superkid was. At least they thought they did.

About that: What a bunch of dopes. You didn't need Noah's brains to see that the kid himself had zero action-hero potential. He couldn't walk across a football field without tripping over one of the chalk lines on the turf. It proved that people would believe anything. And not just kids—the principal, the superintendent, the chief of police, the mayor.

But don't knock it. If everybody wasn't gullible, we never would have had this golden opportunity.

We waited for the last superkid fangirl to type her contact info into Noah's phone and press it lovingly into his hand. Then we cornered him in the boys' room.

"Oh, hi, Daniel. Hi, Daniel."

Sanderson started the conversation going. "We're going to do you a big favor, Noah."

"It's okay," he told us. "You don't have to. Everybody wants to do me favors now. Sophie Lewin bought me mini Oreos at lunch today, and I didn't even ask for them. I only eat regular-size Oreos."

Nussbaum took over. "You're going to want this favor. It's a good one. We're going to do you the favor of not telling anybody who the real superkid is."

His usual innocent, clueless expression disappeared in a hurry. He turned pale, but since he was pretty pale anyway, the color was closer to concrete gray.

"What do you mean?" He was as good at lying as he was at cheerleading.

"Noah," Sanderson clucked. "You know we know. We know Donovan is the superkid, and you were only in the neighborhood to pick a fight with Hashtag."

"Nice outfit, by the way," Nussbaum put in. "Especially the painted-on boots."

"Just imagine how upset everybody would be if they found out," Sanderson went on. "Think about the kids. Think about Sophie Lewin. She might want her Oreos back."

"She can have them!" Noah panicked. "They're in my locker! I didn't eat them—they were the wrong size!"

"Don't worry," Nussbaum soothed. "Your secret is safe with us. But Daniel here"—indicating Sanderson—"you know he loves to talk. Don't freak out. He won't. But keeping something that huge inside is going to be hard. So you'll have to do something for us in return."

"Anything!" he promised. "Just name it."

"Our homework," Sanderson replied readily. "We'll email it every day after school. You can send it back when it's ready."

"Donovan says the classes here aren't challenging enough for you," Nussbaum added. "Maybe this'll help. Extra—challenge."

Noah looked relieved. "Thank you. I won't let you down."

We both frowned. Maybe we should have asked him for more.

Having a certified genius doing our homework didn't turn out to be as good as we thought it was going to be. Don't get us wrong, it definitely had its advantages— like the fact that we didn't have to do it ourselves. But it wasn't perfect.

It was no big deal for Noah. He was so smart he could do it blindfolded. Within half an hour of the end of cheerleading practice, there it was on our iPads. He didn't even email it. It just magically appeared as if we'd done it ourselves.

"It's relatively simple," he explained. "I hack into the school's server, and from there, gain access to your individual devices." He added disapprovingly to Sanderson, "I don't think one-two-three-four is a very secure passcode."

But there were problems. The written work didn't sound like us. It sounded more like someone who knew what he was talking about. Worse, it sounded like Noah, which meant it didn't sound like anybody on earth. Eventually we realized we were spending more time dumbing it down than it would have taken us to do it the normal way.

The math and science went better, except that our teachers were finding it hard to believe that we always had the right answers without showing any work. Noah never showed work because he didn't do any— all the calculating happened at light speed inside that goofy head of his. But the teachers thought we were copying from somebody else. We denied it, which was technically the truth. We weren't copying; we weren't doing anything at all. But we knew from Donovan's experiences at the Academy that suspicious teachers were bad news.

Something had to give. The whole point of getting out of homework was getting out of homework, not doing more just to cover up the fact that we weren't doing it.

"Face it," Nussbaum said. "The guy's *too* perfect."

How could you get normal homework out of a guy who was so über-smart that it was no problem for him to hack into the school computer and beam our assignments directly into the memory of our iPads?

"He hacked into the school computer!" Nussbaum exclaimed suddenly.

Sanderson made a face. "What a brainiac."

"Don't you get it?" Nussbaum insisted. "We black-mailed him into doing our homework so we could get good grades. We don't have to do that anymore."

"But if you don't hand in your homework, you get *bad* grades."

Nussbaum shook his head. "Think! If you can hack into the school computer, you can get any grades you want!"

And a plan was born.

The next time we cornered Noah in the bathroom, we told him the good news: He no longer had to do our homework.

He looked scared. "You're not going to tell everyone about—you know—the thing?"

"Of course not," Sanderson assured him. "Your secret is as safe as ever—*if* you do us this one little favor."

"I already did you a favor," he protested. "The homework was the favor."

"The next time you hack into the school computer," Nussbaum began, "we need you to go to the grades part and punch ours up a little."

Noah looked disapproving. "You shouldn't want that. Oh sure, I could give myself an F in English or Math, but that would be meaningless. If I get an F, I want to have *earned* it."

"Yeah, but we want the opposite of that," Sanderson told him. "You know, A's and B's."

"It's not going to be satisfying," he warned us.

"So you'll do it?" Nussbaum prodded.

"It's not so simple," he explained. "That part of the website has a much higher security protocol. I'd have to create a bot."

"Bot?" we both asked at the same time.

"An internet program designed to gain access to the restricted sections. Then, with a randomly generated password, you'll be able to enter the site and change your grades yourselves. Although," he added, "you know my opinion on that."

We looked at each other, and the sheer triumph practically crackled in the air between us. Even though we asked, I don't think either of us believed Noah could actually do it. Not because he wasn't smart enough, but because—well, it was just too good to be true. Being able to remake your report card was like being given the keys to the kingdom. You didn't have to worry about tests, essays, projects, research, quizzes, class participation, homework, or any of the things that affected your grades because only one thing affected your grade: you, and whatever keystroke you chose. It was paradise.

And it never could have happened without Donovan.

They had it right in kindergarten. Nothing was more important than having friends.

# 14

# SUPER K.I.S.S.
## DONOVAN CURTIS

Something I never would have believed possible: Noah was getting weirder.

Fame was doing it to him. He had played many roles in his life: genius, nerd, outcast, robotics whiz. None of these had prepared him for what he had to deal with now: celebrity.

When he walked down the hall, people scrambled to get near him, high-five him, fist-bump him, be noticed by him. He was constantly being asked to relive the moment he performed his heroics. With each retelling, the story became more daring, hair-raising, death defying, and downright miraculous.

He posed for so many selfies that he was late to every class. But that was okay. The teachers worshipped him almost as much as their students did. The school newspaper published a special Superkid issue, and the yearbook devoted a double-page spread to him. A letter to the *Post* even suggested that the building should be renamed Hardcastle-Youkilis Middle School. Dr. Schultz promised to take it up at the next board meeting.

The Daniels loved it—mostly because they enjoyed watching me squirm.

"That's got to hurt," Nussbaum commiserated, all the while grinning like an idiot. "You know, watching somebody else get famous for what *you* did."

"Yeah, it should be Hardcastle-Donovan Middle School," Sanderson added in sympathy.

"Not so loud!" I hissed. "Okay, so it bothers me a little. But it's better than everyone finding out it was me."

Even Noah's fiercest critic—Hash Taggart—was warming toward the local hero.

The same Hashtag who'd been about to pound

Noah into hamburger if Beatrice hadn't chomped him. Hashtag—the only reason Noah had been on Staunton Street that fateful morning in the first place.

Suddenly, the injured lacrosse star's face began to appear in the crowd that was always around Noah. Every day at lunch, Hashtag moved a space or two closer at Noah's cafeteria table. When a sixth grader pushed ahead of Noah in line for the drinking fountain, Hashtag practically body-checked the poor kid halfway down the hall. Whether he wanted one or not, Noah had a brand-new BFF.

The kinder, gentler Hashtag applied to Noah only. He was still off the lacrosse team, still playing wounded warrior with his big fat arm in a sling and blaming me for it. As soon as that big fat arm was out of the sling, he promised, he would use it to teach me a lesson I wouldn't soon forget. At least, that was before the superkid talked him out of it.

"You're lucky Noah likes you, man!" he told me. "Otherwise you wouldn't get off so easy for siccing your hairball on me!"

Another reason why I was getting mercy was that the lacrosse team was on a winning streak, despite the absence of their star. What was their secret? The superkid. He was an inspiration. And since Noah was a cheerleader, he was always on the sidelines to lift their flagging spirits.

That was another thing about Noah's new fame. Nobody seemed to notice what a terrible cheerleader he was anymore. Brad always complained that celebrities had a free pass at life. They weren't held to high standards, the way soldiers and sailors and marines were in the military. Well, that was exactly what was starting to happen with Noah. Nobody said anything bad about him these days. His praying-mantis posture was now "laid-back," and his whiny voice had become "emo." He wasn't short anymore; he was "compact," or "feisty." And his bizarre personality was described as "unique" or even "alternative."

"Alternative to what?" Nussbaum mused innocently. "Human?"

"Martian," Sanderson corrected.

"You take that back!" came an angry voice from behind us.

We all turned around. The cheerleaders were coming out of the locker room on their way to practice. There stood Vanessa, hands on hips, glaring at us. "How dare you make fun of Noah? You're not fit to carry his pom-poms!"

"With a little weight training," Nussbaum returned,

"maybe Noah could be strong enough to carry his own pom-poms."

Her eyes shot sparks. "You're a jerk! If it wasn't for Noah, poor Megan would be dead!"

Megan came up beside her. "Can people stop saying that? I might have survived, you know." Then her expression turned angry and she added, "But you *are* a jerk! All three of you! You pretend to be Noah's friends, and as soon as he's not around, you bad-mouth him! Noah, who's so"—her face twisted—"great."

I'd seen hints of it before, but this was the first time it sank in that our beloved cheerleader-in-chief was getting sick of being told twenty times a day that she owed her life to the kid who kept knocking over her human pyramid. Megan, who should have been more grateful to the superkid than anybody, really couldn't stand the guy.

She just couldn't say it out loud.

I couldn't get a sense of what Noah himself thought of all this. He had no time for me. He had friends and girlfriends—girlfriend wannabes, anyway. I tried staking out his locker a few times. It was covered in Post-it notes of congratulations, with pink envelopes drenched in perfume jammed into the air vents.

When I did find him there, he was always surrounded by admirers.

Outside of school, he was just as hard to pin down. He had interviews. Thanks to that appearance on *The Russ Trussman Hour*, the story of the superkid was starting to go beyond Hardcastle, and his parents picked him up almost every day to whisk him to some newspaper office or radio or TV station. When the Youkilis family Prius was parked in the school's circular drive, it caused more excitement than a sighting of Air Force One.

When he was at our house visiting Tina, he was too busy for me. Katie was following through on her promise to turn him into a better cheerleader. Day after day, Brad took Tina out for a walk in her carriage so his wife could work with Noah in the backyard. It was a lost cause. He couldn't do a cartwheel or a somersault. He couldn't balance on one leg for more than a second or two. He could throw a punch and yell, "Fight," but not at the same time. He wasn't even good at clapping.

Every so often, Brad would parade by on the sidewalk, straight-arming the frilly pink carriage in front of him like it was a battering ram he was about to smash through some enemy fortification. The sight of Noah flopping all over the grass trying to jump or kick or dance was almost painful to him. Each time he circled by, his deepening exasperation had turned his face a little grayer.

"It's a lost cause," I couldn't help but blurt on one pass.

"There's no such thing!" He pushed the carriage into my arms. "Take the helm."

He strode across the lawn and stopped right in front of Noah, who was on the ground after yet another failed cartwheel.

"Atten-*hut*!" Brad barked.

To my amazement, Noah scrambled to his feet and actually stood at attention, his arms straight against his sides.

Katie laughed. "All right, Brad—"

"Dismissed," he told her.

"Very funny, but Noah and I are working on—"

*"Dismissed,"* he said, with more authority this time.

And she backed away a step.

Noah let out a nervous giggle, which he swallowed when Brad addressed him again.

"Cheerleader, you lack balance, basic coordination, and physical confidence. From now on, this neighborhood is your parade route, and I am your commanding officer. Is that clear?"

Noah tried to look at Katie, but she avoided his eyes. "Well, uh—"

"The proper response is 'Yes, sir!'"

"Yes, sir," Noah managed, totally cowed.

"Outstanding." Brad wrapped the strap of Tina's diaper bag under Noah's arms and around his shoulders so that it hung like a backpack. "Forward, *march!*"

And off they went down the sidewalk, with Brad counting, "*Hup*, two, three, four. *Hup*, two three, four . . ."

As they passed, Noah shot me a pleading glance, which I answered with a helpless shrug.

"Eyes front!" Brad snapped.

Even my baby niece seemed fascinated by it all, but she was still too young to sit up in the carriage and watch her crazy father. Maybe that was for the best.

I rolled Tina back to her mom. "Don't you think we should rescue poor Noah?" I asked Katie.

She looked thoughtful. "Maybe Brad's onto something."

"Seriously? Marine training for the cheerleading squad?"

She shrugged. "Let's give Brad a chance. He can't do any worse than I've been doing."

It was almost an hour before they appeared again, two specks on the horizon—one four times the size of the other. The "hup, two, three, four" wafted in on the wind. Brad was still going strong, but Noah was dragging. He was red-faced, panting like an old dog in a heat wave. And yet—was it just me, or did he look a little better, marching almost in rhythm, his shoulders back? At least they would have been, if he had shoulders. Okay, it wasn't perfect posture, but at least it was posture.

When they finally got back, he collapsed onto the front steps, hyperventilating.

"You did great, Noah," Katie approved.

"Outstanding," Brad agreed, removing the diaper bag from Noah's back. "Same time tomorrow."

Noah didn't have enough breath to respond.

I figured we'd never see him again. I mean, *I* was stuck with Brad. He was family. But Noah didn't have to put up with this. He was the superkid—at least, everybody thought he was.

Yet the very next day, after cheerleading practice, there he was at our door. And the day after that, and so on. On the fourth day, I looked out my window to see Kandy frolicking in a huge truck tire that was lying in the grass of the backyard.

Uh-oh. Brad was getting creative. Noah was in for it now.

And when Noah couldn't budge the truck tire, much less flip it, Brad took one of the wheels off his SUV for his cadet to train with.

Noah was dubious. "Couldn't we just march some more?"

"We'll do that later," Brad confirmed. "Marching is outstanding for cardio, but tire flips build strength and endurance."

"Well, it's just that the average light truck tire weighs thirty-five pounds," Noah persisted. "That is, depending on tread wear—"

Brad cut him off. "Atten-hut!"

Noah scrambled to attention. If I didn't know better, I would have sworn his back was straighter than it had been just a few days ago.

"Cheerleader, if you can't flip this tire as far as that fence, you're not fit to carry the pom-poms of the Hardcastle Middle School cheerleading squad. Is that clear?"

"All right." Noah sighed. "I mean, yes, sir."

By this time, trainer and trainee had an audience—Katie, Tina, Beatrice, Kandy, and me. It took a lot of struggling—not to mention Brad barking encouragement all the way—but Noah actually managed to get the tire across the yard. By the time he made it, he barely had the strength left to high-five Tina's tiny hand.

"Outstanding" was Brad's opinion.

My brother-in-law had plenty more in store for his trainee—push-ups, sit-ups, jumping jacks. Noah did eleven. Not of each; in total—one push-up, three sit-ups, and seven jumping jacks, depending on whether or not I should count the one where he got his feet tangled up and fell flat on his face. Jumping rope had to be scrapped because the cord kept wrapping itself around Noah's neck.

"Outstanding," Brad said again.

I had to admit that watching a guy strangle himself with a jump rope *was* kind of outstanding. Meaning it definitely stood out in your memory.

I felt sorry for Noah, but then it dawned on me. My brother-in-law hadn't woken me up for a pre-dawn run ever since the beginning of Noah's Marine training.

Brad had someone to torture and it wasn't me.

The only one-on-one time I ever got with Noah these days was on those minibus rides to the Academy for robotics class. And then he spent most of the time on his phone, checking his Twitter feed.

I put my hand on his shoulder. "Noah—"

"Mmmm." He continued to thumb the small screen.

Louder. *"Noah—"*

"Hey, my tuna melt from lunch got a hundred and fourteen likes."

Eventually, I got so sick of being ignored that I ripped the phone out of his hand and jammed it into his backpack.

He was annoyed. "I was looking at that, you know."

"That's the problem, Noah," I snapped. "Nobody should care about your tuna melt."

"But they *do*. And I got a lot of retweets for my root beer float from Scoops Ahoy. Two twenty."

"Because you posted it in the first place," I insisted.

"It's not my fault I'm famous."

That made my blood boil. "It *is* your fault! It's a hundred percent your fault!"

"You guys okay?" the driver tossed over his shoulder.

"Fine," I replied. If you didn't count the fact that I was on the verge of strangling this brain-dead genius.

I dropped my voice to a whisper. "Everything was going fine until you got the brilliant idea to whip out that St. Christopher medal and tell the world you're the superkid."

"I did that for *you*."

He sounded so sincere, so wounded, that my anger died down a little. "I know you did—at first. But look at yourself now. Your whole life is a blur of high fives and selfies and people liking your tuna melt. And you've gotten so into it that you're forgetting the fact that it *wasn't you*."

"Of course I know it wasn't me," he defended himself.

"Okay, but don't deny that you're loving every minute of it."

"Fine. I like it—a little."

"A little?" I pressed.

"A lot. But what's so bad about that? And anyway, even if I wasn't the one who jumped into the cab of the truck, I'm still the superkid in a way."

I stared at him. "How do you figure that?"

"People read about me in the newspaper or see me on TV," he explained, "and they feel good. Kids see me in the hall or get to shake my hand, and it's the best thing about their day. What difference does it make if I'm not the actual person who saved the house? People think I am. They don't have to be *right*; they just have to believe it."

I actually groaned at that one. Maybe part of Noah's smarts was that he could talk himself into anything.

"The point is," I went on, "you're going to blow it."

"How?" he challenged.

"By talking too much. They don't teach this at genius school, but the key to every good lie is K.I.S.S."

"Kiss?"

I nodded. "It stands for *Keep It Simple, Stupid.* Every time you retell the story, every interview you give, you run the risk of messing up a detail."

"Impossible," he scoffed. "I have an eidetic memory—that means I never forget anything."

I shook my head. "You never know when you're going to get asked something different, something you're not ready for. Sure, you were on the scene, but you weren't inside the truck. Once a reporter sniffs that something's not kosher, it's all over. No one will let it go until the truth comes out."

I was pleading. If all this came unraveled, it was bad news for me and even worse news for Beatrice. But it would be pretty awful for Noah too. For the superkid to be exposed as a phony would be a total disaster. He'd be ruined in Hardcastle. His family would have to move away and start a new life someplace else. Around here he would forever be the guy who lied so that everyone would think he was a hero.

And what was his response? "I am incapable of making that kind of mistake."

"Yeah?" I challenged. "So how come Chloe knows?"

"Don't be silly. How could she know?"

"She just does, Noah! She told me! She's smart! And she's got more common sense in her little finger than the two of us combined. Lucky for us, she's keeping her mouth shut." I didn't mention the part where I spilled the beans and Chloe threw it back in my face. It still stung—although it's probably for the best that she didn't believe me.

For the first time, Noah appeared a little rattled. "Who does she think the superkid really is?"

"Nobody. Her theory is the truck missed the house on its own, and Kaminsky imagined the whole hero thing."

He smiled smugly. "So maybe Chloe isn't as smart as you say."

How come I could see the walls closing in and Noah couldn't?

\* \* \*

We weren't at the Academy five minutes before Oz dropped the bombshell. "Listen up, people. We've got three weeks to get Heavy Metal into shape."

There was a gasp in the robotics lab.

"Three weeks?" repeated Abigail Lee in horror. "But the competition isn't until next year!"

"That's right," the teacher agreed. "This isn't for competition. Hardcastle is hosting the governor next month, and Dr. Schultz wants the best of everything we've got on display at the big assembly. Heavy Metal is going to be the star of the show."

"Why's the governor coming to a dump like Hardcastle?" I asked.

Mr. Osborne grinned. "You've got your friend Noah to thank for that. The assembly is in honor of the superkid. The governor is coming to present him with the State Youth Award for Valor and Community Service."

There was a smattering of applause, but nothing like the adoration Noah was getting at regular school. Awards were no big deal for the Academy kids, who were all here because they were awesome at something—and probably more than one something. At home, their closets were stuffed with trophies, ribbons, medals, and certificates. That was what it meant to be gifted—not that I could relate personally.

I caught a scowl from Chloe, who thought the whole thing was a hoax Noah and I had cooked up together. I had to admit life would be simpler if she was right. Even though I didn't want any credit for being a hero, for some reason, it bugged me that Chloe believed I didn't have what it took to be one. We were supposed to be friends.

"Heavy Metal won't be ready in three weeks!" Abigail protested.

"Nonsense," Oz told her. "Obviously, our project won't be in condition to compete in an actual meet. But all Heavy Metal has to do is present the governor with a Hardcastle Independent School District tote bag. Then we'll give a short demonstration of the robot's capabilities and our part will be done. Simple."

In order to participate in next year's competition, Heavy Metal had to be able to shoot small projectiles at targets, deploy a miniature drone, and perform a variety of tasks for the judges.

The teacher added, "There's extra credit in it for all of you."

Normally, Abigail was the world's biggest fan of extra credit. But in this case, her gifted reasoning didn't like the risk-reward curve. If our robot screwed this up, the governor would go straight home and email Harvard, Stanford, and MIT: *Whatever you do, don't give a scholarship to Abigail Lee.*

"It's not right," she complained. "We've deliberately been taking our time because we thought we had until next year's meet. Now we have to rush things, and that's never good."

Oz was cheerful. "Welcome to the real world, people, where your boss wants everything yesterday, and you've got no choice but to deliver. Consider this your first life lesson. Noah, how are you coming along with the latest update for the robot's operating system?"

"Well," Noah began, "I've been really tied up lately with all the media attention. Plus my cheerleading responsibilities . . ."

That was a surprise. We weren't used to hearing excuses from Noah. He could split the atom, play chess against supercomputers, map the genome of a banana, and still have enough time left over to watch family pets drinking out of the toilet on YouTube. When it came to Noah's capabilities, there was no such thing as no such thing.

Then again, Noah wasn't exactly himself these days. Literally.

Oz went on, briefing Abigail, Chloe, Latrell, Jacey,

and the others on what they needed to do to bring Heavy Metal up to speed in time for the governor's visit. They listened with total focus, like the gifted students they were. Since I was mainly the joystick operator, my role would come later.

My eyes were on Noah, who was barely paying attention, gazing blankly out the window like he was daydreaming. It was something I expected from myself, not from Noah.

Somehow, being the superkid was transforming the most gifted of the gifted into a regular dummy like me.

"Would Donovan Curtis come to Principal Verlander's office immediately, please? Donovan Curtis to the office."

When I heard my name over the PA system a couple of days later, I was blindsided. Not that it was unusual hearing myself called to the office. My name had been spoken over that PA so many times that I felt I deserved a little plaque on the base of the microphone.

What had I done *lately*, though? Okay, saved the Mercury house, but nobody knew about that. And if the truth had gotten out, the news wouldn't be coming from any principal. It would be coming from Brad, who would have just surrendered his beloved dog to

Animal Control. I'd hear him coming too, because he'd be in his tank, and there'd be a sign on the turret: SMILE, DONNIE.

I entered the reception area and automatically started for the principal's office. But the secretary stopped me and waved me toward the small conference room on the opposite side.

"He's waiting for you in there."

Really? Why would Verlander need to use the conference room? Were they bug-bombing his office or something?

Then I entered the conference room and I knew. It wasn't the principal at all. It was Channel 4's own Russ Trussman.

The sight of him sent an electric shock up my spine. What did a TV personality want with me? The answers I could see were all bad. He interviewed Noah last week—this had to have something to do with that. But surely even Noah wasn't crazy enough to leak our secret to someone who made his living broadcasting stories to hundreds of thousands of people. You didn't trust a guy like that with a secret. To him, there was no such thing.

"Russ Trussman, Channel 4. Good to meet you, Donovan."

He held out his hand and I shook it, noticing that his shirt cuff stuck out of his sleeve exactly the right amount, revealing a cuff link that was a shiny golden *T*.

"What do you want with me, Mr. Trussman?" I asked nervously.

He leaned forward, sticking his famous face into mine. "Can *you* think of any reason I'd come to see you?"

"Uh . . . no?" It came out as a question even though I tried really hard not to say it that way.

"Your friend Noah interviewed with us last week, and I don't have to tell you how impressed we all were."

He paused, and the way he did it made me feel like I was expected to contribute to the conversation. Maybe it was an interviewer thing. So I managed, "He's an impressive guy—that's for sure."

"So I asked Mr. Verlander if I could swing by and talk to some of Noah's friends. You know, get the story behind the story."

"What's the story behind the story?" I croaked, my mouth suddenly very dry.

Trussman smiled with all thirty-two teeth. It was practically blinding. "We all know what the super-kid did, but my viewers want more. They need to *understand* him—who he is, what makes him tick, what drives him to put his life on the line to save people he doesn't even know?"

"Maybe he's—impulsive?" That was what everybody always said about me.

"Funny," the television personality mused. "He doesn't strike me that way. He's more the introspective type."

"Well, you know—always expect the unexpected," I offered.

He leaned in even closer—man, I hated that. His eyes bored into my skull like twin lasers. "So what you're saying is, as his friend, that you're not surprised Noah had the right stuff at the right time."

An icy hand clutched at my heart. *He knows,* I thought. At least he knew about Noah. I could only pray that he didn't know about me.

I tried to speak, but no sound came out. The Daniels called this my "fatal flaw." I was quick to action, but not so quick to come up with a good lie to protect myself.

"Well, thanks for your time, Donovan." The smooth TV host pumped my hand again. "Oh, one more thing. Do you have any information about the folding chair that was found in the Mercurys' pool? It's the one piece of this puzzle that doesn't seem to fit."

I shook my head, and Trussman said, "No, of course not." He might have been a good enough reporter to smoke out the fact that Noah was no superkid, but no way could he identify the WWE prop Noah had brought along to bolster his wrestling qualifications for a confrontation with Hashtag that had never happened. Not even Sherlock Holmes could have figured that one out.

He gave me his card in case I thought of anything and sent me back to class. I made it halfway down the hall and collapsed over a drinking fountain, the pounding of my heart echoing in my ears.

I'd been hoping Noah could play hero for a while, and then the whole thing would die out and be forgotten. There was no chance of that now. A professional news reporter smelled a story. And he wasn't going to go away until he found it.

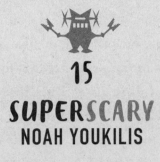

## 15

# SUPERSCARY
## NOAH YOUKILIS

There was a difference between being famous for your IQ or your nationally-ranked science fair project and being just plain famous.

I'd been both, and I had to say that the second kind was way better. Even Dr. Frederick Sanger, who won the Nobel Prize in chemistry twice, wouldn't stop traffic on Hardcastle Avenue. Sir Isaac Newton wouldn't be the star of his cheerleading squad just by picking up his pom-poms. And Stephen Hawking never had a sandwich named after him at the Olympiad Deli like I did (the Superkid: a hero roll with sliced top sirloin and American cheese). I also had a sundae named for me at the ice cream place, and there was a Youkilis Special at the laundry—super-starch for the superkid. Not even Albert Einstein ever got that.

Donovan said it was all fake because I didn't really do the thing I was so famous for. But he was wrong. I saw this YouTube video once called "America's Celebrity Culture." According to the guy, at a certain point, you stop being famous *for* something, and from then on, you're famous *just for being famous*! If that was true, then it didn't matter if I was the one who saved the Mercury house or not. Being the superkid was what I *was*.

Donovan kept warning me that it was all going to collapse like a house of cards. I pointed out that, on a perfectly flat plane, in the total absence of wind and other disruptive forces, a house of cards could theoretically stand forever. Then he got mad, and that bothered me a little, because he was holding me up and some of my fellow cheerleaders were waiting to take me to lunch.

"I have to go," I told him. "If the girls and I don't make it to the cafeteria in time, we won't get our usual table."

"You're not listening, man," he argued. "That Russ Trussman guy—he definitely smells a rat. And he's a professional newsman. Digging up dirt on people is all in a day's work for him!"

I glanced over my shoulder, where Vanessa and the others were checking their phones and looking impatiently at the hall clock. To be honest, I felt a little torn. Donovan was my friend, but the girls were my friends too. Just because I hadn't known them as long didn't make them any less deserving of my attention. After all, when I first met Donovan, I was only Noah Youkilis. Now I was the superkid, and everybody wanted a piece of me.

So I said, "You don't understand, because you're not popular. But I really do have to go."

And as I started for the cafeteria with my new friends, Donovan just stood there in the hall, staring at me with his mouth hanging open.

I guess I gave him a lot to think about.

Donovan was right about one thing: That reporter, Russ Trussman, wouldn't leave me alone. Even though my interview was last week, the host of *The Russ Trussman Hour* kept coming to see me, both at home and at school, and calling me too.

He wasn't very good at taking notes, because he kept asking the same questions over and over again, especially about the chair. To be honest, it was starting to cut into my personal life. Before, that wouldn't have been a problem, because I had no personal life. But now I was really busy. I had cheerleading practice every day, plus extra training with Lieutenant Patterson, which was going really great. I'd improved 700 percent in the number of push-ups I could do, and I hardly fell at all during jumping jacks. In tire flips, I was up to two and a half lengths of the backyard before Lieutenant Patterson canceled them because his SUV needed new brakes. Our marches were now three miles long, with three bricks in the bag over my shoulder. Katie said if I continued to improve, we'd have to switch to a leather duffel because Tina's diaper bag wasn't strong enough for any more bricks.

I also had interviews with other reporters, who weren't so obsessed with one little folding chair. People wanted to honor me, like the governor, who was coming to town soon. I was invited to parties—Megan's for one. I needed cooler clothes—at least that was what Vanessa and the other cheerleaders said when they took me to the mall. I couldn't believe how many different bathing suits they made me try on.

I had to admit there was science in their approach. By logic, until all the possibilities had been tried on, it was impossible to determine with certainty which suit looked best. Vanessa had a very orderly mind.

Russ Trussman even interviewed the cheerleaders, mostly about our routines, and if they contained any moves that might have prepared me for jumping into a moving truck. The girls were also getting kind of sick of Mr. Trussman and his endless questions.

I could relate! It was great to go on TV and all that, especially on a show as popular as *The Russ Trussman Hour*. But I was starting to wonder if it was worth it.

He asked me about the chair at least ten times. He grilled my parents about what time I'd come home that morning, and whether or not my clothes had been wet. Once, he walked me out to his car and asked me to turn the wheel. But the car was in park, so the wheel was locked.

"Interesting," he mused. "So how did you turn the wheel of the propane truck?"

"I shifted into neutral."

He leaned forward eagerly. "You never mentioned that before."

"The detail is self-evident." I added, "How come you need to know all this? Are we doing a follow-up interview on your show?"

He smiled. "Follow-up—that's a good word, Noah. Yes, I definitely think a follow-up is in order."

I wasn't sure I wanted to do another interview with Russ Trussman. To be honest, he was turning into a pain in the neck.

We celebrities had to budget our time.

Another drain on my time were the two Daniels, who'd blackmailed me into creating an internet bot that would enable them to hack into the school computer and change their grades. That level of cyber-incursion was difficult to fit in between interviews, mall trips, and cheerleading practice. I was very relieved to finally give them the program I created, GradeWorm.

That should have been the end of it. But three days later, they lured me into a stairwell, their faces lined with worry. D. Nussbaum reached out and pressed something into my hand. It was the memory stick I'd loaded the bot software onto.

"Oh, I don't need the flash drive back," I told him. "I have two hundred more in my closet."

"Take it!" D. Sanderson hissed. "We don't want it!"

"Yes, you do. When I gave it to you, you said it was the greatest thing in the world."

D. Nussbaum put an arm around my shoulders and steered me away from the parade of students going up and down the stairs. "We tried it out last night at home. As soon as we got onto the school site, the warnings started. Security alert. Firewall. Restricted data. Do not enter!"

"I told you about that," I reminded him. "The system generates those responses, but GradeWorm is designed to punch right through them. All you have to do is keep clicking *Ignore*."

"We did," D. Sanderson insisted. "But the messages kept coming. And they got meaner and scarier. If the school finds out we did this, we're dead meat."

"Take it back," the other Daniel added. "Erase it. Maybe burn it. Yeah, that's a good idea. Just having it in your pocket is enough to get a guy expelled. Better yet, throw it into that lake of lava from *Lord of the Rings*."

"What about our deal?" I persisted. "I did what you asked."

D. Sanderson shrugged. "Fine, whatever. We weren't going to rat you out anyway. What kind of lowlifes do you think we are?"

I almost replied, "Very low," but I wasn't sure if there were different degrees of lowness. So I said, "All right," and they scurried off.

I weighed the memory stick in my hand. What was I going to do with GradeWorm? Certainly not erase it. It was a unique piece of coding, elegant in its ability to evade security scans and burrow through firewalls.

But the two Daniels were right about one thing. It would be disastrous to get caught with it. I could get kicked out of school. I'd have to go back to the gifted program.

No. Never.

I had to upload this software to a location where no one would ever think to look for it. A flash drive was too obvious. And my home computer wasn't safe either. I was a celebrity now, and my fame could make me a target for hackers.

And then it came to me. The perfect hiding place.

# 16

# SUPERSALESMAN
## DONOVAN CURTIS

**N**oah was right when he said I didn't understand what it was like to be popular. In fact, I understood exactly zero about Noah these days. When I first met him he was an oddball genius with an IQ so high that even the Academy brainiacs regarded him with awe. Now he was a hero, a cheerleader, the "it" guy at school, and flirting with remedial classes.

I barely recognized him. Vanessa and the cheerleaders had been taking him to the mall to punch up his wardrobe. They'd convinced him to get prescription sunglasses, so half the time you couldn't see his eyes under the flat brim of his 59Fifty baseball cap. I wouldn't have known him at all if it wasn't for the way his new clothes hung off his praying-mantis frame. That wasn't something you could change with a trip to Hot Topic or Aéropostale.

This was the guy who thought you could create wrestling boots by spray-painting the skin-tight ankles of your skin-tight long underwear.

Then again, how could I understand? I wasn't popular.

That remark still made my blood boil. Before all this superkid business, I'd been the only thing standing between Noah and death by dodgeball. If it hadn't been for me—with a little bit of help from the Daniels—he would have been wedgied and hung from the flagpole. I took a punch in the jaw from Hash Taggart to protect that ungrateful little jerk-face. And my life hadn't been the same since.

Speaking of Hashtag, he was Noah's new best friend. I guess that made me Noah's *old* best friend. The superkid only hung out with cool people, and I didn't make the cut. It was starting to drive me crazy that *I* personally had bumped Noah up to a level where he could exclude me.

The news had just come in that Hashtag was officially out for the rest of lacrosse season. Even though Beatrice's bite hadn't broken the skin, it had supposedly damaged the muscle underneath it. Sidelined by injury, the captain was supporting his team through the Hornets Booster Club. If he couldn't break records on the field, he would break the record for selling more T-shirts, hats, sweatpants, and pennants than anyone had ever sold before. Wherever kids had money—the cafeteria, the book fair, the pizza place in the strip mall next door—there he'd be, pushing his stash of Hornets stuff. His best customers were the sixth graders, who were the youngest, the smallest, and the most afraid to say no. And because it counted as school fundraising, the teachers let him get away with it.

It had gotten to the point that Hashtag's foghorn voice had become an expected interruption to the usual lunchroom buzz. "Hey, everybody, I see a lot of you out there who haven't had a chance to pick up your gear yet!" Or: "School spirit, baby! Support the green and gold!"

I cringed into my chicken nuggets. Everybody knew what was coming next.

"Here's a guy who shows his Hornets pride! Give it up for the Youkinator!"

Oh, how I hated that nickname.

Hashtag reached down and hauled Noah onto the table beside him. The superkid was decked out in team apparel, from his Hornets slouchy beanie to his green-and-gold athletic socks and matching flip-flops.

A roar of appreciation went up in the cafeteria. All those students who'd been hoping Hashtag would shut up and go away mobbed the table, thrusting money at "the Youkinator."

"Oh great, now he's hawking T-shirts," muttered a voice behind me.

"His first celebrity endorsement," I added in disgust, before turning around to see Megan at the table next to mine.

We looked at each other, both of us regretting our words—or at least who we'd said them to.

I couldn't help noticing how comfortable Noah seemed to be, as he perched on the tabletop accepting handshakes and high fives while Hashtag conducted business. What had happened to the clumsiest kid in the world? Surely it wasn't Brad and his Marine training. Aside from a few tire flips and push-ups, all they were doing was lugging a diaper bag full of bricks around the neighborhood.

It drove me nuts when my brother-in-law went on and on about the wonderfulness of his beloved Corps. But what other explanation could there be?

I turned to Megan. "Has his cheerleading gotten better?"

"You must be joking!" she practically spat.

I shrugged. "A couple of weeks ago, he would have fallen off that table and knocked himself unconscious. Now he's almost—nimble."

"Maybe," she admitted grudgingly. "He says he's taking extra lessons with this former cheerleader."

"Katie Patterson," I supplied. "She used to be Katie Curtis."

Megan's brow furrowed. "Why does that name sound familiar?"

"She's my sister, for one thing."

Megan shrugged it off. "Yeah, well, whoever she is, she must be the klutz whisperer, because he's definitely better. Not that it's possible to be any worse."

I was about to confess that the real klutz whisperer was the United States Marine Corps, but at that moment, Noah's high-pitched voice piped, "Special superkid deal—five dollars off all sweatpants! Comfortable enough to throw yourself into a runaway truck and save Megan Mercury from getting killed!"

Her stony expression could easily have been carved on Mount Rushmore.

I couldn't resist. "You might have survived," I whispered.

"Yes!" she exclaimed. "That's what I keep telling everyone, but—" All at once, she caught herself. Glaring at me, she gathered up her lunch, and carried her tray to a table on the opposite side of the cafeteria.

Funny—for a minute before she stormed away, I could have sworn that Megan had been about to crack a smile in my direction.

Robotics lab. Governor's Simulation, Take 1:

Heavy Metal crossed the robotics lab, his hydraulic lifting arms bearing a tote bag like the one he was supposed to present to Governor Holland. I manipulated the joystick to put him into the final turn.

The robot continued in a straight line, past the stacks of equipment and worktables.

Latrell was playing the part of the governor, his hands out to receive the bag. "Is that supposed to happen?"

I wiggled the controller back and forth. Zero response from Heavy Metal.

"Shut it down, Donovan," Oz ordered.

I flipped the kill switch on the joystick unit. Instead of stopping, the robot bumped into a desk, changed direction slightly, and rolled on toward the far side of the lab.

"Shut it down," Oz repeated.

"I'm *trying!*"

I dropped the controller and ran after the malfunctioning robot. I was faster, but Heavy Metal had a head start. As I reached out for the emergency shutoff on the robot's side, a spark shot from the switch to my index finger, shocking me. I jumped back, and watched as Heavy Metal smacked into the wall. The lifting forks punched matching divots in the drywall and only the fabric of the tote bag stopped the entire body from breaking through as well. As Heavy Metal keeled over on its side, a rear flap popped open and an avalanche of golf balls rat-a-tatted onto the floor with a sound like machine gun fire.

Abigail screamed. She always took robot fails personally.

Everyone converged on the scene. Noah got there first. For a moment, he actually kept his balance, dancing deftly on a sea of moving golf balls—props to Brad and his Marine training. That thought had barely crossed my mind when Noah's legs flew out from under him and he went down with a crash. Okay, maybe not.

I reached out a hand to steady Chloe, who was about to be next, and the two of us picked our way over to Heavy Metal. By this time, the power was off and the Mecanum wheels had stopped spinning. Oz was on his hands and knees, rubbing his shoulder. The rest of the team were either scattered like ten-pins or standing frozen, afraid to take a step as the balls continued to roll, spreading like an oil slick.

"Why does it have to be golf balls?" I complained in the horrified silence that followed. "What's wrong with Ping-Pong balls? At least when you step on those, they break."

The answer made me feel stupid, which happened a lot at the Academy.

"Ping-Pong balls are too light," Chloe explained. "Their trajectory would be affected by air currents. It would be impossible to calibrate the firing mechanism."

Chloe and I helped our teacher pick up the robot and set it upright.

"No permanent damage," Latrell commented after giving Heavy Metal a once-over.

"If you don't consider the wall," Oz put in mournfully. "We already have the highest budget in the whole school. This isn't going to look good on my expense report."

"But what went wrong?" Abigail demanded.

What she really meant was whose fault was it? If it was a structural defect, that pointed to Latrell and his team, who'd built the physical body of the robot. If it was a computer hardware problem, Abigail might be responsible. If it was software, the culprit would be Noah. If the source of the glitch was hydraulics or pneumatics, that sounded a lot like Chloe. And if it was an "operating issue," you could slap the cuffs on the dummy with the joystick.

I suggested, "Maybe the controller ran out of batteries. That happens all the time in video games."

Thousands of IQ points in the room, and I was the only one who thought of that—including Oz.

"Well, it's easy enough to check," the teacher decided.

So we did. The batteries were perfect. And the blame game started over again.

"People! People!" Oz waved his arms for quiet. "We're a team, remember? It doesn't matter whose fault it is! The only important thing is that we get it straightened out! Which we will—*together*!"

"We're going to look pretty stupid if this happens in front of the governor!" Latrell put in.

"Thank you!" Abigail exclaimed. "Only we won't just look stupid. It'll be a black mark on our records."

"You know, your record is just other people's opinions of your performance at things that were never very meaningful in the first place," Noah told her soothingly.

She almost bit his head off. "That's easy for you to say! You have the highest IQ in the state, and you're the superkid!"

Every now and then, something reminded me that there were definite advantages to being ungifted. This was one of those moments.

"Calm down, everybody," Oz ordered. "This isn't the first time we've ever had issues. We'll fix this."

He was trying to be reassuring, but nobody was reassured.

The whole point of a controller was to be in control. When the robot ignored all commands and rolled off on its merry way, you weren't in command anymore.

What was wrong with Heavy Metal?

# 17

# SUPEREXCITED
## MEGAN MERCURY

I should have noticed that Shayna Rodgers didn't look as solidly upright as she normally did. But I was at the top of the pyramid, beaming straight out into the bleachers, a textbook dazzling smile on my face. The smile was mandatory, even though this was only practice. Ms. Torres always said to make the smile a part of the routine. If you always wore it, when game time came, you would never forget.

They told me later that when the pyramid crumpled,

I smiled all the way down. I was proud of that—and proud of Vanessa and the girls on the bottom level, who caught me just before I hit the ground.

But that didn't explain what had gone wrong. "What was *that*?" I demanded, turning on my cheerleaders.

They seemed pretty rattled too. The human pyramid was our trademark move. It was second nature to us by now.

"Take it easy, Megan," Ms. Torres soothed. "That's why we practice. To get everything just right."

"We shouldn't have to get the pyramid right," I argued. "It's been part of our routine going on three years. We should be able to do it in our sleep!"

"Relax," our coach insisted. "There's no such thing as absolute perfection. No matter how good you are, and how hard you train, at some point you're bound to slip up. It just happens. Nobody knows why."

"*I* know why" came an all-too-familiar voice.

Vanessa stepped forward. "What is it, Noah? What did we do wrong?"

The other girls jumped all over this—like being interviewed on *Russ Trussman* made you a cheerleading expert.

"It's simple physics, really," Noah explained reasonably. "Weight ratios. I can fix it for you if you want."

"Listen, Noah, we've been doing this for a long—"

Vanessa cut me off. "He can fix it!" She had stars in her eyes.

"Certainly," he said. "I just need everyone's individual body weight—in kilograms, preferably."

A roar of outrage went up in the field.

"Pounds would be okay too," Noah put in quickly. "I can convert in my head."

"Let's take a break," Ms. Torres advised. "I'm sure the pyramid will be fine from now on."

The girls headed for towels and water bottles.

Noah went over to a young woman who was sitting in the first row of bleachers, watching the practice. It occurred to me that this must be Donovan Curtis's sister—that ex-cheerleader/master of lost causes who was trying to work with Noah.

When I saw her, I did a double take. Her face was burned into my memory. Katie Curtis—no wonder I knew that name!

I was in kindergarten, maybe pre-K, when the cheerleaders from Hardcastle High came to our school to give us a demonstration on field day. I never forgot the show they put on. Flying through the air and then somehow landing perfectly—and with a smile, too. Those girls—so pretty, so athletic, so self-assured. They were the center of attention, and they gloried in it. I made up my five-year-old mind on the spot that I would be exactly like them one day. Especially the head cheer-leader—and there she was years later, leaning over the bleachers speaking with Noah. Katie Curtis.

I had to thank her for inspiring me. The minute Noah went into the locker room, I rushed over there. I could feel my heart pounding—like I was about to meet the president, or Taylor Swift, or some major celebrity.

I promised myself I'd play it cool, but once I was in front of her, it all came pouring out of me, and I gushed through the details of that field day all those years ago.

Katie Curtis—Patterson now—seemed a little scared at first. As in *Who is this stalker?* Once she real-ized what I was babbling about, though, she was really nice. "I can't believe you remember that!" she told me. "I barely remember it myself."

"It changed my life," I told her earnestly. "I was sit-ting at the end of the row, and when you guys were done, I shouted, 'I love you!' And you stopped and gave me a big hug right in front of everybody. And I'll never forget what you told me. 'Kiddo,' you said, 'keep those pom-poms moving.' I still use that to this day. When I'm cheerleading, if my arms ever get tired, it's your voice I hear. And I find a tiny bit of extra strength." I stopped, suddenly embarrassed, and added, "Sorry for being such a fangirl."

She grinned. "Are you kidding? These days I'm sleep deprived and buried in dirty diapers. I need all the fans I can get. Like Noah—although he's really more a fan of my daughter."

"Right—Noah." There it was. I couldn't even share a moment with my long-lost cheerleading idol without Noah coming up like a bad burp that tasted like yesterday's guacamole. I changed the subject. "I'm really excited about next year. They let the high school squads enter competitions."

Katie nodded with a nostalgic smile. "Great times. We brought home a lot of hardware—trophies and ribbons and stuff."

"I've seen some of it—in the display cases at Hardcastle High. I hope we can measure up to you guys one day." I added, "Got any advice for me?"

She thought it over. "Well, the first thing you have to do is get the bugs out of your pyramid. Listen to Noah. He's a genius!"

I read somewhere that it was never a good thing to meet your heroes. They always let you down.

* * *

As the semester rolled on, the lacrosse team kept on winning, even though Hashtag was still on the bench. The temperatures stayed chilly, the spring rains lingered on—until the magic date approached. My birthday.

My dad called it Megan's Luck. Suddenly, the skies were clear, and the weather got hot. Perfect conditions for swimming. Rah, rah, global warming! I was so excited about my upcoming party that I was finally getting my cheerleader's positivity back.

I was stringing patio lights on the section of fence that had just been repaired while the guy from the pool company checked the pH levels of the water. The two of us were alone out there. Mom, Dad, and Peter were inside the house with Russ Trussman from Channel 4. Of all the people who were making a fuss over the whole superkid business, he was the grand poobah. We were so happy to have our fence back and our pool back. When were we going to get our lives back?

The answer seemed to be: whenever Russ Trussman found something else to talk about on his TV show.

I was tying the end of the string of lights to the corner post when he came wandering into the backyard,

202

grinning at me with all those teeth.

"Just a few more questions, Megan."

Right—in addition to the nine hundred he'd already asked. "Fire away." Ms. Torres would have been proud of my cheerleading smile. Especially when what I really wanted was to ruin his perfect hair with the bug dipper.

The notebook came out. I was starting to hate that notebook. "I understand you're on Noah's cheerleading squad."

"No," I said, trying to keep the ice out of my voice, "he's on *my* cheerleading squad. *I'm* the head cheerleader."

"What I can't get my mind around," he went on, "is why Noah would do such a heroic thing and then run and hide. Especially since the two of you are such good friends."

"Well, Noah's really modest," I murmured.

"Really?" He raised two perfect brows. "I don't get that impression at all. If you ask me, I'd say he's even gotten a little carried away with the spotlight. He loves the attention. Which begs the question: Why did he shy away at first when the whole town was looking for him?"

He had a point, and I probably would have given it

some serious thought if I cared—which I didn't. Who could guess what drove Noah? He was like a roll of the dice. Anything could come up.

Aloud, I said, "He's on my squad, but I really don't know him that well."

The reporter took out his phone, tapped the screen a few times, and held it up. The video showed a lacrosse field at halftime, with the cheerleaders performing. We were all in tripod formation, looking really together.

Then Noah came along. He took the feet out from under Claire, clocked Judy with an elbow, and came within a few inches of stomping on my face after they dropped me. It was almost as painful to watch as it had been to survive the first time around. But the worst part was the crowd. They barely even noticed that Noah had ruined our routine and had nearly put his sneaker-prints on my forehead. They were rooting for their superkid, chanting his name while I lay flat on my back, with the wind knocked out of me, hyperventilating through what was left of my perma-smile.

I could feel my eyes narrowing at the TV reporter. What was his angle? Was he trying to trick me into saying Noah was a lousy cheerleader so he could make me look ungrateful on *The Russ Trussman Hour*?

"Some of his cheer skills are a work in progress," I

ventured carefully. "He's gotten better."

"Skills can be taught," he told me. "But jumping in the window of a moving truck—that takes natural athleticism. Some of us have it." He paused the video on his phone, freezing Noah in mid-stumble. "Some of us don't."

I stared at him. "You don't believe Noah did it! You think it was somebody else!"

He didn't say yes or no.

"You're dreaming!" I laughed. "It was Noah, all right. One hundred percent."

"How can you be certain?" he asked.

It just slipped out. "Because I couldn't get that lucky."

There. I said it. I would have given anything for the superkid to be someone else. Dracula. Jabba the Hutt. Some intelligent moss from outer space that came to Earth on the tail of a comet.

*Anybody.*

Russ Trussman pocketed his phone, flipped his notebook shut, and started for the gate. "Thanks for your time, Megan. See you Sunday."

"Sunday?" I echoed. "I'm busy Sunday. It's my—"

"I know, your birthday party. I'm coming back with a camera crew to shoot the superkid's return to the place where it all happened. Great human interest angle—at least, that's what your mom said."

And he was gone, leaving me standing there with smoke coming out of my ears. Bad enough I had to invite Noah. Now Channel 4 was going to turn my birthday into a celebration of his super-ness. And my own parents were in on it.

*Go, Mom and Dad.*

"All done, miss."

I was so lost in my misery that when the pool guy came up behind me, I almost took off like a rocket.

"Oh—uh, great," I managed. "Thanks."

"I found this in the filter." The guy handed me a bright purple doggie toy shaped like a hand-weight. When I took it, the thing emitted a waterlogged squeak.

"I guess your dog lost it," he added. "Funny name for a dog."

"We don't have a dog." I turned the plastic toy over in my hand. Across the plastic was printed: KANDA-HAR.

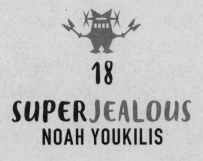

# 18

# SUPERJEALOUS
## NOAH YOUKILIS

There's a principle of radiation physics called decay. All radioactive material slowly loses its radioactivity. It never drops to zero, but it constantly diminishes according to a formula called half-life.

I was beginning to believe that decay applied to friendships, too.

When I first met Donovan, my life was an endless loop of learning, understanding, internalizing, and predicting. He showed me that knowing a lot was fine, but it was overrated. I needed unpredictability, randomness, fun.

So, like the radioactivity of an isotope, our friendship would never go all the way down to zero. But it was getting harder and harder to keep it up.

Donovan had changed. He was angry at me for being the superkid. Didn't he remember I was doing all this for him? I tried to get him to come forward and take credit for being a hero. He wouldn't do it. He was too worried about being caught in Hashtag's neighborhood. And when I saw how worried he was about being caught, I did what any good friend would do. I stepped in and took the pressure off him. No one would look for a superkid if they already had one— me. How was I supposed to know how great it was going to be?

A know-it-all would have known. But that was the old Noah. I wasn't such a know-it-all anymore. I got a D on my salad bowl. I was being considered for remedial classes.

Besides, there had been no data to analyze, no scientific method to follow that would have enabled me to predict how awesome I was about to become. Or that I would love it as much as I did.

Just walking through the halls at school, the air

practically crackled with ions at two or even three times their usual positive charge. When I made eye contact with someone, it was like a spark from a Van de Graaff generator. Girls left sweet-smelling notes in my locker. Guys wanted to be my friend. Hashtag was talking about running me for student body president as a freshman next year in high school. It was paradise.

There was only one problem: Donovan.

"But, Noah"—we were on the bus—"can't you see it's all based on a lie?"

"I see that it *started out* based on a lie," I admitted. "Now it's based on the fact that I'm the superkid."

"Which is a *lie!*" he insisted.

"Not at all," I explained. "The lie is that I saved the Mercury house. Saving a house is something you *do*, and I didn't. Being the superkid is something you *are*. And I am."

My theory was that—even though Donovan didn't want to be the superkid himself—he resented the fact that my life had become fantastic and his was still nothing much. I hadn't had much experience with jealousy before now. At the Academy, all anyone cared about was grades, or summer internships, or awards, or IQ points. I always had the most of all those things, so I was out of the envy loop. But at Hardcastle Middle

School, I was starting to see what a corrosive emotion jealousy could be.

"It's not jealousy, you little maniac!" Donovan rasped at me. "You're riding so high that you're bound to screw up and say the wrong thing! Especially to that Trussman bloodhound! And then we're both toast."

I was kind of insulted that he would think that I couldn't handle myself around a few harmless questions. Donovan had the idea that Mr. Trussman was trying to trip me up. Nothing could have been further from the truth.

No one appreciated the superkid more than Mr. Trussman. Not even the Hardcastle papers had given more attention to my story than *The Russ Trussman Hour.* He visited our house so often that Dad had started to joke about charging him rent. He'd even stayed for dinner a couple of times. He was like family. And not just to us—the Mercurys invited him to bring a camera crew to Megan's birthday party. Mr. Trussman was going to do a special on my triumphant return to the place that made me famous.

For some reason, that really freaked Donovan out. "Don't you get it? He's *stalking* you! You've never been to a party in your life. Your guard will be down, and you'll let slip something he shouldn't know! Please,

Noah, stay away from that party."

"I can't," I told him honestly. "I promised Megan I'd be there. She's my head cheerleader. She'd be devastated if I didn't come. I'm the most popular person in our entire school. I know that sounds like fun and games to someone like you, but it's also a big responsibility. If I don't show up, the whole party will be a flop."

Then he said something really mean. "If your 206 IQ meant anything more than a locker combination, you'd know that Megan Mercury would rather see you at the bottom of the ocean than poolside at her birthday party."

"Megan *likes* me!" I protested.

He stared me down. "She doesn't, Noah. She pretends to. But to her, you'll always be the guy who ruined her cheerleading squad."

I was outraged. "I'm a *great* cheerleader!"

He shook his head. "You've gotten better. You might even get to be good someday. But you're never going to be a great cheerleader."

I forgave him for that, because it was just the jealousy talking. I could see, though, that it was the beginning of the end for our friendship. My superkid status had brought me a lot of happy moments. When I looked to the future, I saw so many good things ahead, like being famous and having a lot of friends. But standard probability analysis told me that Donovan wasn't likely to be one of them.

I missed him already.

Megan's party was scheduled for noon. But I didn't want to be late, so I got there at 11:05 just to be on the safe side.

"Happy birthday!" I announced at the door, and she looked at me like I had two heads. I added, "Is that what you're wearing to your party?"

"These are my *pajamas*, Noah. You're a little early. Can't you, you know, go someplace for a while, and come back when the party's supposed to start?"

"Okay," I agreed. "Where do you want me to go?"

She turned bright red, but didn't offer any suggestions.

"Here!" I thrust my gift bag into her hands. "It's a biography of Dr. Robert Oppenheimer, also known as the father of the atomic bomb."

"Just what I always wanted," she said flatly.

I walked around the neighborhood for a while, but there was a queen bee that kept chasing me, and I had a bad allergy to stings from pollinating insects.

So I knocked on Hashtag's door.

"Youkinator!" he greeted me. "Come on in, man! The guys are here!"

He was talking about Zane and a couple of other lacrosse players. They were invited to the party too, since they were also popular, like me.

Hashtag ushered me into the living room. "Yo, look who I found!"

"Superkid in da house!" hooted Zane, and everybody high-fived me.

This happened to me all the time now that I was famous.

"Make yourself comfortable, Youk," Hashtag invited. "We're just doing a little pregaming."

"There's a game?" I was alarmed. "What about Megan's party?"

As it turned out, pregaming just meant hanging out before a party, because "only losers show up early."

This was another thing I never could have learned at the Academy, even though the curriculum there was supposedly so advanced.

The guys were playing something called Bangladesh, which had more to do with punching people than with the real country in Asia. One player would declare, "Bang la —" followed by the name of a body part, like "Bang la chest" or "Bang la knee," and then he would hit the other person in that spot. As the superkid, I didn't have to participate, but I said I would, because I didn't want special treatment.

I got "Bang la stomach," and Zane punched me so hard that I couldn't breathe and I almost threw up the cereal I had for breakfast. Then everybody got mad at Zane and I couldn't tell them I was okay because all the wind was knocked out of me.

"But guys—I barely touched him!" Zane pleaded. "I was going easy!"

It took three of them to hold Hashtag back from attacking Zane. "You could have hurt the Youkinator!"

"Just a diaphragm spasm," I managed to croak, "brought on by a blow to the abdomen that put pressure on the solar plexus."

"Yeah, well, whatever it is," Hashtag seethed at Zane, "don't ever do it again!"

But as angry as everybody was, they all made up when it was time to hide the smashed china figurines that had been on the coffee table I fell over.

Hashtag kept asking me if I was sure I was fine. I don't think Donovan was ever this concerned about my welfare. Hashtag even said we couldn't play

Bangladesh anymore, because it was too dangerous. Then everyone got bored really fast, so we decided it was time to go to the party.

By this time we were a little late, which was okay because Hashtag liked to make an entrance when the party was already in full swing. Since I was the super-kid, my entrance made his entrance even better. The camera crew from Channel 4 filmed the whole thing, and Russ Trussman made all the guests sign release forms if they wanted to be on TV with me. Everybody signed.

I'd never been invited to a party before, so I'd spent the past week researching them on YouTube. It wasn't very helpful, though, because there were so many different kinds of parties—tea parties, costume parties, political parties, Tupperware parties, toga parties, sleepover parties—a plethora of parties, in fact. There was one party in Texas where everybody had to ride a mechanical bull. I hoped Megan didn't do that here. My solar plexus still hurt.

Mostly, this was a swimming party, although it could also be considered an eating party—mostly pizza and chips and a big birthday cake. Megan blew out the candles, but I didn't eat my piece, because what if she sprayed?

I was hoping to avoid going in the pool, but the girls made me. So many of them had helped me pick out my bathing suit, and they insisted on seeing it in action. I did okay in the shallow end, but pretty soon, Shayna and Vanessa tugged me out into the middle. When I tried to touch bottom with my toe, I went under. I inhaled a lot of water and started choking and flailing around. My memory is a little hazy on what happened next, because of the panicking and all that. There was definitely a lot of yelling. Vanessa wailed, "He's *drowning!*" and someone—possibly Hashtag—bellowed, "The Youkinator went under!"

A voice a lot like Megan's screamed, "Dad—do *something!*"

There was a gigantic splash, and a second later, Mr. Mercury was dragging me over to the side. He boosted me up onto the pool deck, climbed out himself, and pounded me on the back until I stopped wheezing.

I said, "Hey, *you* saved *me* just like *I* saved *you!* Isn't it amazing how life comes full circle!"

Obviously, Mr. Mercury wasn't much of a philosophy fan. He turned long-suffering eyes on his daughter. "You *could* have let me take my phone out of my pocket before you pushed me in, honey."

"What else could I do?" Megan defended herself. "He was *ruining* my party!"

"I get it," I told her, teeth chattering a little. "Irony. Worrying about a party when someone's life might be in danger."

"If you say so," she muttered under her breath.

Mr. Trussman got a little suspicious after that. "You can't swim?"

"It's not among my capabilities," I confirmed.

His gaze narrowed. "Then how were you able to get out of the truck when it was in the pool?"

But I wouldn't be ensnared so easily. "When I climbed through the cab window I was able to reach the side of the pool. Then I just hoisted myself up."

Mr. Trussman gave me a long look and wrote it all down.

# 19

## SUPERSPLASHY
### DONOVAN CURTIS

"Donnie . . . Donnie . . . *Donnie!*"

That got my attention. My sister Katie stood over me, baby Tina in her arms, the way LeBron James carried a basketball. "Why don't you answer me? I've been calling for ten minutes!"

"Sorry," I mumbled. To be honest, my mind was across town on Staunton Street, at Megan Mercury's pool party. Noah was there, and so was Russ Trussman. A whole afternoon for the reporter to trick Noah into saying something stupid. "What's up?"

"Have you seen Kandy's bowwow bone? I've torn the whole house apart looking for it!"

I shrugged. "Who cares? A new chew-toy costs— what, three bucks? What difference does it make?"

"Oh, none at all," she said sarcastically. "If you don't count *this*!"

I looked up. In her free hand she held the white hat of Brad's Marine dress uniform. The shiny black brim was mangled and twisted beyond recognition. "Without his bowwow bone, Kandy chews everything he can get his teeth around! Brad's going to hit the moon!"

I nodded wisely. "And he'll make Noah march there with him."

"Don't be mean, Donnie. Brad's done amazing things with Noah. He's a whole new kid now."

It was a sore point. I liked the old kid better. For one thing, the old kid wouldn't be at Megan's party, spilling his guts to Russ Trussman. That could be happening *any minute*!

I couldn't just sit on the sidelines. I stood up and kicked into my sneakers.

"Perfect," she exclaimed. "Walk away from me. I've got plenty of time to go to the pet store and pick up a bowwow bone. It's not like I've got a new baby who feeds constantly and never sleeps."

"Tina's a great sleeper," I tossed over my shoulder. "It's the rest of us who keep waking her up."

This was my second sprint to Staunton Street to avoid a disaster. The hill didn't make it any easier, but at least Megan's house was on the downside of the slope. Panting, catching my breath, I took note of the bikes and skateboards on the front lawn. I could hear laughter, excited chatter, and water splashing. This was party day, all right. Megan's pool parties were legend at Hardcastle Middle School, not that I'd ever made the guest list.

Cautiously, I scooted around the side of the house, taking note of the chipped brick where the tanker's side mirror had broken off. The fence was back up, but the gate was open. Inside was a solid wall of kids in bathing suits—dancing, horsing around, and having a great time. It was exactly what we outsiders had always imagined Megan's shindigs to be like. More important, it was crowded, which meant I might be able to get myself close to Noah without being identified as an uninvited party-crasher.

I spied Megan on the lawn at the center of a group

that was sword fighting with brightly colored pool noodles. And there was Noah. Uh-oh—Trussman was with him, a microphone thrust under Noah's chin, while a cameraman filmed everything. I had to get over there!

A series of food tables had been set up in a line. I dropped to all fours and began to crawl under them. Reaching the end would put me as close to Noah and Trussman as I was ever going to get. I had no idea what I planned to say to them. My only purpose was to break up the interview. Maybe the sight of me up close and personal would be enough to remind Noah to watch his mouth.

I scrambled out of my tablecloth tunnel so intent on reaching Noah that I didn't notice the hefty frame that stepped in to block my way.

"Curtis." Hashtag's iron grip locked onto my shoulder. "What are you doing here, man? You're not invited."

I played the only card I had. "Well, yeah, but Noah really wants me."

The injured lacrosse star shook his concrete head. "Nice try. Noah's real disappointed in you, man. He told me. He still likes you, but you haven't been a great friend to him these days. And anyway, it's not up to him to invite you. It's up to Megan. And she didn't."

"Just let me talk to him," I pleaded.

Hashtag didn't give an inch. "I don't want this to get ugly—I promised my dad out of respect for your brother-in-law in the service. But you're not staying. Go home to your vicious dog."

What could I do? I turned around and headed for the gate. Not that I was giving up, but staying at the party wasn't an option anymore.

As I passed the sundae bar, I reached into one of the topping bowls, grabbed a fistful of peanuts, and jammed them into my pocket. It was the beginning of Plan B.

I ducked into the yard of the Mercurys' next-door neighbors. It wasn't my first time there. This was where Noah and I had ended up after hopping the fence on superkid morning. I remembered there was a big knothole in one of the wooden slats. The two of us had crouched there, soaking wet and shivering, watching the propane truck sink to the bottom of the pool. From there I had a full view of the yard and the entire party. I could even see Noah and Trussman on the opposite side of the pool deck. It would have been perfect—if I could read lips. The problem was I couldn't hear them. There was too much background noise between their interview and me. I had to get closer. But how was that going to happen with Hash Taggart on the prowl?

That was when I noticed the low-spreading elm tree that dominated the yard. It was gigantic—it must have been here fifty years before there were any houses on Staunton Street. One gnarled branch extended up over the fence and out across the Mercury property.

Even while I was climbing up the trunk, I had a vague sense that I was starting on something that the Daniels might one day call a Donovan Classic. Sure, I knew it could turn out badly. But there was also a chance that it would totally work. Regardless, I had to hear what Noah was telling that lousy reporter. That part was mandatory.

About fifteen feet up, I reached the branch and began to shinny out over Megan's yard. It was a lush elm, with plenty of leaves to hide my presence. If anybody looked up, hopefully they wouldn't notice there was a guy perched there, spying on the party.

The limb rose at first. Then there was a knobby intersection where the main branch dipped and extended over the pool. As I crept forward, I kept an ear out for conversations below. At first, it was just a muddle. When I concentrated, though, I could pick out individual voices. It was hard to miss Noah's nasal twang—especially when I pushed on close to the very end of the branch. I was directly over the pool now. There weren't too many kids in it because three girls were performing a synchronized swimming routine. Megan's little brother bobbed close by, sunning himself on an inflatable float.

Trussman was still interviewing Noah. They stood on the far side of the water, no more than fifteen feet from my position. I locked in on their exchange, straining to make out every word.

"What do you remember about the interior of the propane truck?" Trussman was asking.

*Don't answer!* I screamed in my head. *It's a trap!*

I couldn't very well shout a warning, so I did the next best thing. I reached into my pocket, pulled out the peanuts, selected one, and bounced it off the back of Noah's head.

Ha! Bull's-eye!

He looked around in shock, which Trussman interpreted as avoiding the question. "Come on, Noah," he probed. "The way you jumped in, you must have been looking straight down at the seats. What color were they?"

I threw another peanut, this one harder. Noah jumped like he'd been struck by lightning.

"Black? Blue? Gray? Red?" Trussman prompted. "You must remember. You have an eidetic memory. You said so yourself."

This was trouble. Even an eidetic memory couldn't remember what it never saw. *Black!* I exhorted silently. *Black!*

But telepathy didn't work, so I threw a few peanuts this time. One of them must have hit Trussman, because he looked around too.

So far so good. If he was searching for what was pelting down on him, he wasn't asking questions. I was almost starting to enjoy myself—which usually meant something bad was about to happen. But I was too lost in the moment to consider that.

I reached for another peanut—and something warm and furry nibbled at my hand. Startled, I glanced down and almost swallowed my tongue. A giant gray squirrel was on the branch with me, helping himself to my stockpile of peanuts.

I snapped my hand back as if I'd been burned and momentarily lost my grip on the limb. A rain of peanuts hit the pool. At the last second, I managed to grab the branch again, swinging around to the underside. Now I was hanging there in full view of the entire party.

Noah was the first to spot me. "Hey, isn't that Donovan?"

Excited shouts rose from the partygoers.

I couldn't tell if anyone else heard it, but I sure did— the branch made a crunching sound back at the trunk. My squirrel definitely noticed. He beat a hasty retreat out of there, scampering along the top of the fence just ahead of disaster. No such luck for me. Disaster was my middle name.

With a crack, the limb gave way at the giant knot. The end of the branch swung suddenly down, taking me with it. It lurched to a stop at a right angle and I kept on going. I lost my grip and dropped like a depth charge, hitting the water in a spectacular belly flop. The splash must have been visible from outer space.

If there was an Olympic record for synchronized swimmers evacuating a pool, those three girls shattered it. It earned a mocking ovation from Megan's brother, who was still on the raft, bobbing in the waves created by my unexpected arrival. The poor kid had no idea that the broken branch was hanging over him like a diamond drill bit.

I sucked in a lungful of air, kicked off the bottom, and launched myself upward. I broke the surface like an undersea missile, aimed for the Mercury kid, and wrestled him off the raft.

He managed one syllable of protest. "Hey—!"

The hanging branch came down, spearing the float, which exploded with a loud pop. I pulled for the side, towing Megan's brother. I was a decent swimmer, even with my shoes on. I didn't want to think about the condition he would have been in if I'd left him on the raft.

Megan gawked at me as if I'd just dropped out of the sky—which I had.

"Donovan, what are you doing here?" Noah exclaimed. "You weren't invited!"

Leave it to the guy with the 206 IQ to take everything that happened and come up with *that*.

# 20

# SUPERPROTECTIVE
## CHLOE GARFINKLE

<< *Hypothesis: Principals will do anything for publicity.* >>

With the governor's visit drawing close, the super-kid's name was on everybody's lips. Channel 4 News had decided to cover the assembly live on *The Russ Trussman Hour.* Russ had come to the Academy to interview the robotics team about Noah before the big event.

What a joke. I seemed to be the only person in Hardcastle, kid or adult, who could see that Noah was taking credit for something that had happened without any help from him or anybody else. I couldn't even get my own parents to believe that the propane truck must have hit a bump and changed direction on its own, missing that house entirely. Everyone wanted a hero, and Noah was the guy. Worse, my dad actually accused me of being jealous.

<< *Hypothesis: There are a million reasons to be jealous of one of the greatest minds on the planet. This isn't one of them.* >>

On top of it all, we were still having trouble with Heavy Metal, and Oz didn't want to let a reporter into the lab. The last thing we needed was for rumors to get out that our award-winning robotics team was cooking up a dud for the governor. So we got called to the library one by one for the interviews.

"In all the years you've been in the gifted program together," Mr. Trussman asked me, "has Noah ever struck you as being particularly athletic?"

I laughed out loud. "Noah?" There were so many words that could be applied to Noah—brilliant, innovative, peculiar, nerdy, awkward, scrawny. Athletic? Never.

"The window of the propane truck measures thirty-six inches wide, twenty-four inches high, and five feet off the ground. To dive through an opening that size—one that's moving—requires a perfect combination of strength, agility, and timing. You've known Noah for some time. I'm just trying to get a sense of how that remarkable ability evolved."

That was when it hit me. I usually caught on much quicker than this.

*<< Hypothesis: Russ Trussman isn't profiling Noah; he's trying to prove he's a phony! >>*

My first reaction was: Finally, someone else with the brains to see through this sham!

But almost immediately after that, I thought about Noah. This wouldn't be a vague rumor spreading around town that the superkid wasn't quite on the level. This would be a news story on Channel 4 telling everybody that their hero was a fraud. He would be branded a con artist, a liar, and a joke. And his biggest fans would become his worst enemies of all, because he would have made them look so stupid.

Well, tough.

*<< Hypothesis: Noah of all people should be smart enough to know that he can't get away with this. >>*

In spite of that, I felt my lower jaw tightening with determination. It was nothing against Russ Trussman. He was only doing his job. But was I going to help him ruin Noah's life? Not a chance.

I looked Mr. Trussman straight in the eye. "It's amazing what some people can do in a crisis."

He asked a few more leading questions, but I mumbled only yes or no answers. Eventually, he gave up and cut me loose. I returned to the lab, and Jacey headed to the library to face the reporter.

I wasn't sure how I felt about what I'd just done. On the one hand, I'd just protected someone I was pretty sure was duping the whole community. On the other . . .

<< *Hypothesis: You don't sell out your friends.* >>

Back in class, Oz had taken over the controls from Donovan and was trying to get the robot to behave. Sometimes it executed commands perfectly. But every now and then, it was almost as if Heavy Metal had a mind of his own. He'd stop when he was supposed to go. He'd turn left when the joystick moved right. Despite all our brainpower, we couldn't figure out if it was a software problem, a hardware problem, or even an issue with the wireless hub that interpreted signals from the controller.

We just didn't know, and it was driving us nuts. And if the rest of us were frustrated, Abigail was losing her mind. After Noah, she was the smartest on the team.

Knowing was ultra-important to her, so this was more than just a setback. It was an identity crisis. Plus, the governor's visit was barely a week away. Whatever this was, she needed it solved yesterday.

"It's Noah's fault," she complained. "We're going to look like clowns in front of the governor thanks to him."

I regarded Noah, who was at a computer, scanning through endless lines of software code. "Come on, Abigail, why blame Noah? He's just as stumped as any of us."

"That's not the real Noah," she said bitterly. "*He'd* solve this in a heartbeat. That's the superkid, and *he's* too distracted by his own press."

"You know as much about Heavy Metal as he does," I reminded her. "Why don't you fix it?"

"Dream on." She sighed wanly. "As much as I hate to admit it, this problem calls for a super*mind*, not a superkid. And right when we need him most, he's lost planning his next big interview."

She probably had a point, and I couldn't help shooting a stink eye in Donovan's direction for his own role in this hoax. The sooner it ended, the better.

I stepped away from Abigail and came up behind Noah, pretending to be studying the screen over his shoulder. "Russ Trussman is on to you," I whispered in his ear. "He knows you're not the superkid."

He nearly broke his neck searching the lab for Donovan. Donovan, who'd been crazy enough to tell me *he* was the superkid!

"Did Donovan put you up to this?" I probed.

He actually tried to get up and walk away from me. I grabbed him by his skinny shoulders and plopped him back in the chair. "Noah, I'm trying to help. You could get in big trouble—"

Donovan was heading our way, a concerned expression on his face. I spoke quickly. "At this point, it's too late to confess. But after the governor's visit, you've got to stop playing hero and hope all this dies out. And whatever you do, watch yourself around that guy Trussman."

Donovan arrived in time to hear the last part. "What about Trussman?"

"This isn't a game anymore," I hissed. "Trussman smells a rat and—"

I was interrupted by a high-pitched whirring that filled the lab. At the top of Heavy Metal's stainless steel body, a door slid open. We saw the propeller first as the miniature drone rose out of our robot and hovered there over our heads.

All eyes turned to Oz, who had the joystick in his hands.

He shook his head. "I didn't do anything. It just happened."

Everyone on the team understood what that meant. If the robot could deploy its drone with no command from any operator, then Heavy Metal was completely out of control.

We just stood there, staring up at our runaway drone.

"If it won't respond to the joystick," mused Noah, "how are we going to get it down?"

Nobody had an answer for that—nobody except Donovan. He snatched Oz's jacket from its wall peg, jumped up on the teacher's desk, and launched himself into the air. He captured the little craft inside the folds of the blazer, fell lightly to the floor, and handed the coat—drone and all—to Oz.

It got a round of applause from the robotics team.

That had always been the thing about Donovan.

<< *Hypothesis: It can take someone ordinary to perform the extraordinary.* >>

# 21
# SUPERSUPPORTIVE
## HASH TAGGART

Okay, here's my deep, dark secret: My arm was fine. I hadn't felt any pain for weeks. I was totally ready to go back to the lacrosse team.

So what was the problem? I guess I was scared. Not of reinjuring it. Lax was a tough game, but I was a tough guy. At least I thought I was.

The thing was that the Hornets were on a winning streak. They were playing like champions—and without me, their captain. What if I came back and we started losing?

It wasn't impossible, you know. That kind of consistency, game after game—no way could it last forever. But if my return put us into a skid, no one would see it that way. They'd think it was my fault, period. Because I was a showboat or a ball hog or even a jinx. Because I put my shoulder pads left side first, instead of right, and somehow offended the lacrosse gods. Sports fans could be crazy superstitious that way.

Or—and this one really hurt—people might say it was because I had never been as good as I thought I was.

So I stayed on the disabled list. I hadn't worn the sling in a while—people would have seen through that in a heartbeat. I sat on the bench with the players, giving them advice and encouragement. I wasn't an athlete exactly, but I was definitely part of the team, only in a support role. Athletic supporter—hmmm, that didn't sound so good, but you get the point, right? I was being supportive—the way the cheerleaders were.

Funny, I'd never appreciated the cheerleaders before this season. I always thought of them as kind of an accessory for the players, like cool uniforms. You know, something to make us look good. But they were athletic supporters too. They had a coach. They held tryouts. They practiced every bit as much as the players did. They developed routines the way the Hornets worked on new plays.

Megan had always tried to tell me these things, but I guess I never listened. It was the Youkinator who made me take the cheerleaders seriously. And it wasn't just because he was the superkid—although that was a big deal. Being friends with a real-life hero wasn't something that happened to everybody.

Youk may not have had a superpower—but that was what made him so *awesome*. At first glance, he had less than nothing going for him. Yet against all odds, he was the best of all of us. The superkid, sure, but so much more.

Watching Youk as a cheerleader was like watching a caterpillar change into a butterfly. From my spot on the sidelines, I had a front row seat for that. Okay, he was never going to be fantastic, like Megan and some of the girls. Remember, though, Noah used to be the dweeb/shrimp/goober/stick-bug/klutz who knocked down the human pyramid and sent Vanessa to the emergency room. Back then, he reminded me of Beyblade or maybe the Tasmanian Devil—a spinning instrument of destruction that flattened everything in its path. Now he was steady on his feet; he moved in time with the cheers. When there was music, he kept the beat. He was *fine*.

Megan definitely did not agree. "If that's fine, I'd hate to see what you call terrible!"

Despite the fact that Youk had saved her life, she was just about the only person in town who didn't appreciate the superkid.

"Come on, Megan," I argued. "Give the guy a little credit. He used to be a disaster. Now he isn't anymore. You've got to appreciate that. It's easy to be good at something when you've got natural ability. But when you really, *really* stink, and you have to work hard, and never give up, and finally get to be just so-so—*that* takes commitment. That's what it takes to become a hero."

She glared at me. "Oh, please. He's only so-so because *I* changed our routines to keep him at a safe distance," she snarled. "And gave him things to do that even he couldn't screw up."

"Have a heart, Megan. He's a great guy. And not just because he saved your life—"

"*Might have* saved my life," she corrected through clenched teeth.

"Look," I said. "I made fun of him too. I hid his pants in gym class—the whole nine yards. And I was *wrong*. Just because he's weird and skinny and kind of funny-looking and talks like an encyclopedia doesn't mean he isn't as good as anybody. And you know what else? I like him."

She rolled her eyes. "News flash: You're the president of his fan club. If you had a magic wand, you'd turn yourself into him."

"Not true!"

"Look at yourself. You're even *standing* like him—hunched over, your head hanging, your knees bent—"

"I am not!"

"Look!"

She whipped out her makeup compact and held up the mirror. Oh, man, she was right! I threw my shoulders back, stuck out my chest, and straightened my legs. "Well, so what? When you make friends with somebody, you pick up some of each other's habits."

Come to think of it, I'd been noticing a lot of kids, boys *and* girls, looking like that—round-shouldered, kind of stooped. It had to be Youk—not only did we see him around school, but his picture was displayed in store windows, and he was constantly in newspapers and on TV, especially *The Russ Trussman Hour.* He was like a fashion statement—you know, when some celebrity does something and everybody starts to copy it. I called it "The Youki-look."

The funny part was that Noah didn't have the Youki-look so much anymore. As he got better at cheerleading, he also started standing up straighter.

"It's from Marine training," he explained when I asked about it.

You had to love the guy. It was like everything else he said. He might have been joking, but who could tell? Maybe he was talking about some military stuff he found on YouTube. If there was one thing the Youkinator liked more than cheerleading, it was You-Tube.

I used to think that I was popular because I was an athlete, and I hung out with all the right girls, and the cool people. But Youk was the opposite of that— an oddball loner who nobody really knew, and didn't have any friends, except maybe that loser Donovan Curtis. And, true, people only noticed him because he got famous. But that was a while ago. At first, people liked Youk because he was the superkid. Now we liked him because he was Youk.

Soon the governor would be coming to town to

honor him. Governor Holland had never visited Hardcastle before, not even when he was running for office. But in a few short days he'd be in our cafeteria, giving our Youkinator a medal.

That was going to be epic.

## 22

# SUPERREVEALING
## MEGAN MERCURY

**M**s. Torres always taught us that there was a cheer to cover every situation. Your team was down by fifty points? *E for effort! That's how we do! We are proud of you!* Pouring rain for the entire game? *Weatherman, weatherman—you're no good!* The bleachers were on fire? *EMT for you and me! Let's all hear it for the VFD!*

She was wrong. There could be no cheer, no chant,

no routine for a situation where the entire world was upside down.

On Saturday, Governor Holland was coming to Hardcastle to hang a medal on Noah. It started out as a celebration for just our school. But once people like Mayor DaSilva and Superintendent Schultz got wind of it, the whole town was involved. Decorating the cafeteria had become an obsession. No classwork had been done for days. All anybody had to say was, *Can we make more streamers or posters or paper chains for Saturday?* And the teachers would be off to the art room for supplies. Seriously, Earth could have had an extra rainforest if it wasn't for the construction paper we used.

As I walked through the halls, Noah's face beamed at me from every wall. *My* school, where I'd been head cheerleader since sixth grade, host of the best pool party every spring. I used to be *somebody* in this school. Now I was just the almost-victim the superkid had saved, and the most important thing about me was that my house had been there to allow him to become super.

Could you do a cheer for insanity? *Give me an I! Give me an N! . . .*

No. Nothing to cheer about here.

On Friday, the Hornets won their eleventh straight

lacrosse game, breaking a school record and taking first place in the county conference. And did anyone congratulate the players, or the coach, or the goalie, who had a shutout, or Zane, who scored four goals?

Of course not. Instead, the Hornets stormed the sidelines and hoisted the superkid up onto their shoulders for a victory lap. And while that was going on, the rest of my squad cheered louder than they had during the actual game.

That was the last straw. "Oh, please!" I exclaimed in disgust. "You act like he's personally responsible for an eleven-game winning streak! He's never touched a lacrosse stick in his life, and if he did, he wouldn't know which end to hold! He's a cheerleader like the rest of us, except that we're good and he's hopeless!"

They didn't like that. Vanessa stood right up to me. "*You're* the one who always told us that school spirit is just as important as physical ability. Well, Noah has more spirit than anybody!"

"And he definitely gets the crowd excited," Kelsey added, "which is every cheerleader's main job."

"Noah's a great cheerleader!" Vanessa insisted. "Maybe he didn't start out with mad skills, but he's worked really hard, and you give him no credit at all."

"Fine," I conceded. "He isn't as clumsy as he used to

be. That's not saying much. *No one* is as clumsy as he used to be. So, sure, he improved—only because it's impossible to be less than zero."

"You're wrong," Vanessa said seriously. "He could be as good as any of us. You've written him out of all our big routines. Most of the time, he's just cheering by himself thirty feet away."

"Where he can't do any harm." I pointed to her nose. "You know that better than anybody."

She shook her head. "Where he'll never be able to show that he's on our level, because *you* won't give him the chance."

"The last time I gave him a chance, he nearly took your head off."

She looked me straight in the eye. "You always told us that cheerleading was as legit as any sport—that it took just as much ability and drive and commitment. Well, Noah's more driven and committed than any of us. He's ready to show that he's got the ability. Only you won't let him. I'll bet you're not even that grateful to him for saving your life!"

"Hey—no one can be sure that I would have—" I protested.

But Vanessa had already turned her back on me and joined the other cheerleaders, who swarmed around the players toting Noah. It was the biggest celebration of the season so far, and I wasn't part of it.

Her words haunted me. Was it true? Was I really so blind where Noah was concerned? Okay, he'd gotten better. I never said he hadn't. For sure he wasn't falling all over the place anymore. His posture was straighter; his balance was decent; there was a level of confidence in his movements . . .

Was he as good as Vanessa and the others believed— and I was too biased against him to see it?

It was impossible to tell. I didn't watch him on the sidelines, mostly because I wanted to pretend he wasn't there.

So you couldn't go by me. But you couldn't go by the others either—they were such superkid fans that they thought everything he did was perfection.

I needed an impartial judge. But who?

My eyes found Noah in the swirling festivity. He was reaching down from his perch on everybody's shoulders to high-five Katie Patterson in the first row of bleachers. On closer examination, I saw that it wasn't Katie's palm he was slapping; it was the tiny hand of a very young baby in Katie's arms.

It hit me: Katie was Noah's private cheer coach. However much he'd improved, it had to be thanks to her. She had a better sense of Noah's true ability level than anybody.

Could I trust her opinion? As his teacher, maybe she wouldn't be impartial.

One thing settled it for me: Katie was a fellow cheerleader; a fellow *head* cheerleader. Sure, she was an adult now—but once you'd carried those pom-poms, it was like a sisterhood.

I didn't know where she lived, but Donovan was in the school directory. He'd tell me where to find her.

It was Saturday morning. At one o'clock the entire town of Hardcastle would be squeezed into our cafeteria to watch Governor Holland hanging a medal around Noah's pencil neck. At ten-thirty, though, the day looked totally normal. Nice, even—sunny, not too hot. Cheerleaders lived for weather like this, where you could run up and down the sidelines without a) freezing in your miniskirt, or b) sweating into your makeup. Three cheers for Mother Nature!

But there was no game today. My mission began at the Curtis house, so Donovan could point me in the direction of his sister Katie, the Klutz Whisperer. She was the magician who had supposedly made a cheerleader out of the clumsiest dolt ever to hop, skip, and face-plant across a sports field.

I rang the bell at Donovan's address. From inside, I heard a couple of dogs barking. Finally, the door opened and I was startled when Katie herself appeared. She looked kind of frazzled, holding a pacifier into her baby's mouth. Yesterday, I hadn't realized how young the kid was—a newborn, practically.

"You live here?" I blurted.

She nodded. "Temporarily. Until my husband gets a long-term assignment. Megan, right?"

"Right," I said, thrilled to be recognized by my one-time hero.

She sized me up. "Are you looking for Donnie? He had to go to the Academy."

"For Scholastic Distinction?" I finished in amazement. That didn't fit the picture of Donovan *I* had—you know, the kind of idiot who'd dive-bomb a pool party from a tree.

She grinned. "Yeah, it doesn't sound much like my brother. But he's on their robotics team. The eggheads are doing a demonstration for the governor today, and they're working the last-minute bugs out."

"You're the one I actually need to talk to," I told her.

She invited me in and we sat down on the couch.

The house wasn't a mess exactly, but there was a bassinet in the middle of the living room, an infant swing on the floor, and dog toys scattered everywhere. On the wall was a portrait of Katie in a beautiful white wedding dress and a tall, very good-looking guy in a military uniform, and a smaller picture of a much-younger Donovan as a Little Leaguer. The look on his face seemed to say: *I can think of a lot of good uses for this bat, and hitting a baseball isn't any of them.* I'd seen that expression on his face more than once.

"You've been coaching Noah, right?" I began.

"Donnie told me he was a hopeless cheerleader," Katie explained. "So I thought maybe I could help him. But it was a lost cause."

"No—he's gotten better." It hurt to say, but I was never going to get to the bottom of this if I couldn't be honest with myself. "Some of the girls think he's as good as anybody on the squad."

"It wasn't me," Katie admitted. "I couldn't do anything with Noah. That's when my husband took over."

"Your husband is a cheerleader?"

She shook her head. "He's a tank commander in the Marines. They don't do cheerleading. They *march*. For miles. With heavy packs. That's what he and Noah have been doing. It's been like boot camp around this place—push-ups, sit-ups, jumping jacks, tire flips—you name it."

I was blown away. "And it works?"

"It must," she replied, "because he was a total loss when I tried to work with him—Kandy, stop chewing on the playpen!"

She was scolding the weirdest puppy I'd ever seen—light brown, with a bushy tail and giant feet that looked like they belonged on a grizzly bear.

"Boot camp," I repeated. "How would that do anything?"

Katie shrugged. "Don't ask me. Ask Brad. He believes Marine training is the answer to all the world's problems. Kandy—stop! *Kandahar!*"

My head snapped up. "Kandahar? The dog's name is Kandahar?"

Katie nodded. "That's where Brad was stationed in Afghanistan."

My mind traveled back to when the pool guy had pulled that dog toy out of the filter—purple plastic, dumbbell shaped. And the name written across it . . .

That wasn't like Fido or Poochie. How many Kandahars could there be in a town the size of Hardcastle?

How had this puppy's toy ended up in my pool?

"Kandy chews on everything these days," Katie was explaining. "Shoes, carpets, furniture—he's not fussy. He used to have a bowwow bone he loved, but we managed to lose it somewhere."

It was like being struck by lightning. In that electrified instant, I knew exactly who had lost the bowwow bone—and exactly where and how. Donovan had lost it in my pool while climbing out of the propane truck that *he*—and not Noah—had steered away from my house.

Noah wasn't the superkid. It had been Donovan all along!

How could I have missed it? Noah was the last person in the galaxy who would ever jump into a moving truck. Not only was he physically incapable of it; it would never even have crossed his mind to try.

My eyes returned to the photograph of Donovan the Little Leaguer, brandishing the bat with unholy glee. *That* was the face of someone who'd be crazy enough to throw himself at tons of runaway propane without even thinking about the worst-case scenario. I pictured him dropping from the sky into the middle of my pool party. He was exactly the right kind of reckless idiot! And I remembered what had happened a few seconds after that—that same

Donovan tackling Peter out of the way of the falling tree branch.

He wasn't the hero type, not even close. But deep down, hidden beneath his many faults, he'd always had that heroic streak. It had been staring me in the face all this time.

Donovan had saved my family. It was a hard thing to wrap my mind around—mostly because I had to unwrap my mind around the idea that Noah did it.

I had to come to terms with it—I owed my home and family to Donovan the Doofus. Not even a doofus. He was just sort of—nobody. Not an athlete, not a genius, not a ladies' man, not a student council type. It was like being indebted to a filing cabinet, or the flagpole in front of the school.

Only what filing cabinet ever risked its life to protect a house full of sleeping people?

I was suddenly overcome with a wave of gratitude toward Donovan. For the first time, I felt like there really was a superkid in Hardcastle.

"Are you okay?" Katie asked in concern. "You've gone all pale."

"I'm—fine." I got up and headed for the door, nearly tripping over Kandahar. "I just realized I have to be— uh—somewhere."

"Will I see you at the governor's ceremony later?" she called after me. "I think the whole town's going to be there to cheer for Noah."

"For sure," I managed. "I can't wait to see Noah get what's coming to him."

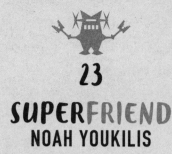

# 23
# SUPERFRIEND
## NOAH YOUKILIS

In his theory of general relativity, Einstein predicted that the fabric of space was actually curved. That was pretty smart for some guy back in 1915, but he missed the most important part. Not only was space curved, but so were cause and effect.

When I was at the Academy, my 206 IQ made me special. I left there to go to Hardcastle Middle School to follow my dream to become average. And it worked for a while. Before long, though, I was the superkid, which meant I was special again. I had followed the curve of cause and effect from unique to ordinary and back to unique.

Which was fine. I hated the way I was tops at the Academy, but being the superkid was fantastic, especially the part where I got to be famous and everybody wanted to be my friend.

And today had to be the very best of a long line of really great days. Today, Governor Holland was coming to town to present me with the state's highest award for youth achievement. Donovan thought this was a terrible idea, because he was the one who'd saved the Mercury house, not me. But as I saw it, human history was filled with examples of people getting rewarded for doing absolutely nothing. Look at all those kings and emperors and sultans and grand dukes who never did anything except get born into the right families. Besides, it wasn't as if the governor asked me if I wanted a medal. He just decided I was getting one. What was I supposed to do? He was the governor.

I wasn't even sure if Donovan was my friend anymore. It made me sad, but there was no more logic in crying over friendship decay than there was over radioactive decay. It was just how the universe worked. These days, Donovan complained about everything

I did. Not like Hashtag, who said it was the governor who should feel lucky for the chance to present a medal to *me*.

"Hold still, Noah." Dad finished tying my tie and folded my starched collar back into place. He clapped the shoulders of my blazer. "Mom and I are so proud. But I hope you realize that we'd be proud of you, superkid or not."

"That's good to know," I said, honestly. It was supposedly both a blessing and a curse to raise an exceptional child like me.

My phone rang. It was Chloe, calling from the robotics lab. The rest of the team had been there all morning. Heavy Metal was still acting up, and time was running out to fix the problem before the demonstration for the governor.

"We've been through every micron of Heavy Metal, and we can't find anything wrong." She sounded exhausted and a little bit scared. "It has to be a software issue."

"I can't come," I told her. "They want me at school before the governor gets there."

There was a scuffle on the other end of the line, and a muffled voice barked, "Give me that phone!" Abigail came on the line. "Now listen, Noah. Heavy

Metal isn't performing, and if you don't get your bony butt down here *this minute*—"

I hung up on her. I once saw a YouTube video called "Keep Negativity Out of Your Life." It seemed like good advice for a big day like today.

"What was that all about?" my father asked.

"Nothing," I replied. "I think we should go to the school now. I want to be early."

We were in the car when my phone rang again. Donovan this time.

"We really need you here, Noah. Everybody's freaking out. Even Oz is losing it a little."

"I'm sorry," I said. "I can't. We're almost at school."

There was a very long pause. Then, "Are you sure you know what you're doing?"

"Don't I always?"

"All right." Donovan sounded resigned. "Good luck."

That made me feel warm inside. Even though we hadn't been getting along too well lately, he was still on my side. "Good luck to you, too," I replied, and meant it. They were going to need it. There really was something wrong with Heavy Metal.

Dad dropped me off, promising to be back with Mom for the ceremony.

The first person I saw was Russ Trussman, who was directing his camera crew as they carried equipment into the cafeteria. He stopped what he was doing and pulled me aside into the empty kitchen.

"Noah, we've got to talk."

"Can't it wait until after?" I inquired. "Dr. Schultz wants me with him when the governor arrives."

He looked me straight in the eye and announced, "I know."

"Right. Well, obviously, the governor is only coming because of me, so—"

"No," Mr. Trussman cut me off. "I mean I *know*. I know you're not the one who saved the Mercury home."

I didn't see that coming. "I—don't understand."

"Come on. You're a nice boy, but you're not exactly hero material. You had no idea that a car has to be in neutral for the steering to be active. You couldn't even explain the folding chair in the Mercurys' pool. Whoever diverted that truck, it wasn't you."

"I can explain the chair," I said quickly. "It was mine. I brought it with me."

He goggled. "Why?"

"For hitting people over the head. You know, like in the WWE."

He stared at me as if I was speaking a language he couldn't understand. "Look, Noah—I can help you, but you have to help me too. First of all, do you know who the real superkid is?"

Well, I couldn't answer that even if I wanted to. I'd promised Donovan to keep his secret.

The reporter got sick of waiting for me to say something. "All right, here's what you have to do. You have to tell the governor that the ceremony is off. It won't be easy, but I'll be there to smooth things out for you. You're not the first kid who ever got caught in a small lie that snowballed out of control. All I ask in return is an exclusive interview. You'll come on my show and explain to my viewers how it all happened. Do we have a deal?"

I might not have been a real hero, but it took a lot of courage not to throw up right there on Mr. Trussman's shoes. More than anything else, this proved that I was right, and that cause and effect really was curved. Somehow, I'd missed the turn that would have saved me from getting stuck in this dead end, with the governor on one side and Russ Trussman on the other.

Donovan had warned me about that from the very beginning. He could see it, even though his IQ was barely half of mine.

I considered the person I'd become, the new Noah, and the good friends I'd made in these past few weeks—people like Hashtag and Zane and Vanessa and the other cheerleaders.

But there was only one Donovan. It was Donovan who'd made the change in me possible—who'd made me realize it was even possible to change.

I felt a surge of fondness toward him.

Then I asked myself: How would Donovan deal with the kind of tight spot I was in right now?

The answer came to me: If Mr. Trussman had solid proof, he wouldn't need me to confess or go on his show or anything. He had his suspicions and otherwise he had zilch. If I just kept my mouth shut, there would be nothing he could do about it.

Through the doorway to the main cafeteria, I could see a motorcade of black SUVs pulling up outside the school.

"I'm going to greet the governor now," I told the reporter. "I'm out of here."

Which was exactly what my friend Donovan would have said.

# 24

# SUPERKID
## DONOVAN CURTIS

The whirlwind around Heavy Metal grew more and more frantic as the minutes ticked down to the one p.m. ceremony. Oz and the team bustled around the hot lab, sweating every bit as much as the athletes who ran cross-country. Screwdrivers opened panels and tightened connections. Soldering guns sizzled, attaching and reattaching wires. Computers flashed through endless pages of code, searching for the faintest sign of a glitch.

As for me, all I could do was watch while my stomach did backflips. I was more scared than anybody, because I was totally powerless. I was just the driver. I had never been a real robotics expert. My eyes flipped back and forth between the clock and Tina's baby picture on Heavy Metal's body. Noah had put it there—Noah, the one person with half a prayer of figuring out what was wrong with the robot. Noah, who could have cracked the case weeks ago if he wasn't so distracted with this superkid stuff.

Noah, who had blown us off to go play hero.

Abigail was bright pink, rattling off the names of colleges that would never accept her if Heavy Metal laid an egg in front of the governor. Latrell was vibrating with tension. Jacey was in tears. Even levelheaded Chloe was babbling high-pitched instructions that she had to know didn't make sense.

Only Oz was calm—although it was a deathly calm, like he had accepted the worst. At 12:45, he said a single word: "Time."

"It can't be time!" Abigail practically yelled. "We're not ready yet! We have to cancel the demonstration!"

"Not an option," the teacher said sadly. "Dr. Schultz has been bragging about the robotics team for so long that the governor asked for us by name." He took a deep breath. "We did ten trial runs and Heavy Metal performed in seven of them. Probability is on our side."

"But there's still a thirty percent chance that he'll screw up!" Latrell protested.

Oz sighed. "There's a *hundred* percent chance that he won't perform if he isn't there. Come on, people, this is a good lesson for all of us. Life can't always be boiled down to a computer algorithm. Sometimes you have to cross your fingers and hope for the best."

*"Hope?"* echoed Abigail. "There's no *hope* in science! It's science!"

The other team members looked on in stunned agreement. In their world, life *was* a computer algorithm, and who needed hope if you had all the possibilities covered? For them, depending on hope was like betting your life on a single lottery ticket.

But by then the bus to take us to the ceremony was pulling up the drive outside the lab door. Ready or not, Heavy Metal had a date with the governor.

Dr. Schultz had hooked us up with the district's "kneeling" bus to make it easier to transport the robot. We carefully guided the Mecanum wheels onto the lifting platform and watched as the stainless steel body was raised aboard. Nobody suggested that Heavy Metal should move under its own power. We were treating this robot like it was filled with nitroglycerine, and could blow sky-high at any second. I didn't have much in common with the big-brained Academy geniuses, but right now, we were all thinking the same thing. We were praying that Heavy Metal could roll across the cafeteria, give Governor Holland his tote bag, put on a little show, and roll back before his next meltdown.

We were almost late because Hardcastle Middle School was a madhouse. The parking lot was jammed, and vehicles clogged the main drive, so we had to go in through the service entrance in the back.

The cafeteria was packed. Every chair was full, and standees four deep ringed the large room. In the VIP chairs at the front, I caught sight of Governor Holland's famous face. Dr. Schultz was also there, and between them Noah. For me, it was a wakeup call that, yes, this was really happening. As much as this chapter in all our lives felt like a bad movie, here was the highest official in our state to remind us that it was all too real, and going down right now. And the blinding floodlights from Russ Trussman's film crew would make sure everyone could see it.

Students were there by the hundreds, not only from Hardcastle Middle, but from all over town. Kids made up about half the crowd; the rest were adults. The superkid had fans—practically everybody had been following the story in the newspapers and by watching *The Russ Trussman Hour.* I spied my parents at a cafeteria table. And there was Brad, his six-foot-four frame elevating him above the rest of the standees. He was right next to Mr. Kaminsky, the driver of the propane truck—who, in a way, was the guy who'd brought us all together today. The Youkilises were front and center, along with the Mercurys. Also the Taggarts—for sure Hashtag wasn't going to miss this big moment in the life of his new BFF. All the Hornets had come with their parents, and all the cheerleaders, too. I even saw the Sandersons and the Nussbaums. The Daniels mugged at me with cake-eating grins—a reminder that they knew who the real superkid was.

There was a buzz of interest as we rolled Heavy Metal onto the scene. Oz flashed a thumbs-up that was supposed to be encouraging but was really kind of pathetic. Anyway, there was no mistaking the anxiety on the faces of his robotics students.

I felt a tap on my shoulder and turned to find Megan standing behind me. Wonderful. Her presence was the only thing missing from my perfect day so far. To be honest, I was surprised to see her there. She seemed like the last person who'd want to show up at a celebration of Noah's heroism. On second thought, what choice did she have? Her house had co-starred in the superkid story.

She was looking at me with an intense expression I couldn't quite identify. She held out something and placed it in my hands. I stared down at the purple plastic. It was Kandy's missing bowwow bone.

"Where did you find this?" I asked, mystified.

"It was in our pool filter," she said in a husky voice, far from the haughty, dismissive tone she always used on the rare occasions when she had to talk to me. "Thank you for saving my house." Then she put her arms around me and hugged me.

Oh, no.

She knew. My eyes shot to Noah. The principal. The superintendent. The mayor. The governor. The hundreds packed into the cafeteria. Oh, Megan—not here. Not *now*!

"I—I—"

"Donovan!" Oz hissed. "We're on!"

Megan released me and I hurried to catch up to the team as Dr. Schultz stepped to the microphone. "Honored guests. Ladies and gentlemen. Students. I think our turnout today says a lot about how a certain young man has affected our lives here in Hardcastle . . ."

Typical Schultz. What a gasbag. Still, as he rambled on about how the superkid's shining example had changed all our lives, I thought of something that had never occurred to me before. Okay, he was talking about Noah, and that was pure baloney. But he was really talking about *me*. *I* was the hero who had not only prevented a disaster but inspired thousands. Me. Donovan Curtis.

When people heard my name, their first thought was *don't try this at home*, not *hero*. I was a mythic screw-up—just ask the Daniels, who were my official scorekeepers. But on that Saturday morning, which now seemed like fifty years ago, I actually got something right—and not a small thing either. I risked my life and saved people. Even Brad's Marine Corps called you a hero for that. I may not have been the superkid, but I was *a* superkid. At least I had been for a single shining instant when my town had really needed one.

The superintendent asked Governor Holland to step forward. My warm, fuzzy moment ended, and the uneasiness returned. It was time for Heavy Metal to do his stuff.

Oz handed me the controller. I stuck the bowwow bone in my pocket and took charge. Breathing a silent prayer, I eased the joystick forward and the robot began to roll.

An *ahhhh* of appreciation went up from the crowd as Heavy Metal moved across the linoleum floor, approaching the chief executive of the state. My hand was none too steady, but I managed to stop the robot at the governor's feet. The lifting arms came up, bearing the Hardcastle tote bag. Beaming with pleasure, Governor Holland accepted the gift and held it over his head for all to see. The audience went wild. Even the people who had managed to find seats were on their feet, cheering not just Heavy Metal, but the award-winning Academy robotics team.

Beside me, Chloe sighed with relief. I knew exactly how she felt—how all of them felt. After so many glitches and so much aggravation, it was starting to seem as if Heavy Metal just might pull this off.

Then I heard the *clunk*.

The governor heard it too, but he didn't recognize the sound for what it was: a golf ball dropping from Heavy Metal's hopper into the robot's launch mechanism.

"Hit the deck!" I bellowed.

For an older guy who was kind of overweight, Governor Holland had quick reflexes. He ducked down just as the ball shot through the spot where his head had been a split second before. The small projectile sailed across the cafeteria and came down in the seats, sending spectators scrambling.

*Clunk! Clunk!*

Another two golf balls were airborne, spraying over the crowd as Heavy Metal spun around on his Mecanum wheels. One shattered the plastic front of the Gatorade machine. The other hit a fleeing seventh grader right between the shoulder blades.

I twisted the joystick and pounded every button on the controller. Nothing happened. Our worst nightmare had come true, and at the worst possible time. Heavy Metal had gone rogue with a hopper full of golf balls in a packed cafeteria.

The robot lurched around the room, firing projectiles in all directions. Cries of shock and pain rang out as golf balls bounced off heads and shoulders. People tripped over each other's feet and ran into one another trying to get out of harm's way.

"Calm down!" ordered Dr. Schultz. "Everything is under control—" A wayward shot swept his glasses clean off his nose. If looks could kill, the entire robotics team would have been dead, starting with Oz.

One ball took out the warming light at the food service line; another cracked the sneeze guard over the salad bar. Brad snatched a third out of the air just before it would have knocked Mr. Kaminsky's teeth down his throat.

Chaos reigned. People scrambled every which way, but the place was so packed that nobody could get anywhere. The governor's aides were draped over him in the middle of the floor, protecting him from harm. Noah crouched under his chair, not very heroically at all.

"Donovan!" Oz cried. "Shut down!"

I raised the controller over my head so he could see me trying to cut power. "Heavy Metal's not responding!"

"We're so dead!" Abigail quaked. "How could it be worse?"

The answer came almost immediately.

Chloe pointed. "Look!"

The door slid open at the top of the robot's body and the miniature drone lifted up over the cafeteria. It hovered there for a moment and then began swooping low over the panicked crowd, dive-bombing heads.

The only word for it was pandemonium. We were being attacked from the ground by a barrage of golf balls and from the air by a runaway drone, all while Heavy Metal barreled around the floor at increasing speed.

Oz ran after the robot, his arms stretched out in front of him. What was he trying to do—tackle it? He had to know better than anyone that the stainless steel body was too bulky to knock over. The team had built it that way on his instructions.

Then I remembered: the kill switch!

I sprinted through the crowd, ducking to avoid the drone, which passed so close that I felt it part my hair.

I did what I always do, without a second thought, because thinking wasn't my big talent. I flung myself at Heavy Metal with every ounce of strength I could muster.

"Oof!"

I landed on top of the out-of-control robot, knocking the wind out of myself and nearly sliding right off. Frantically, I clamped my arms around the body and hung on for dear life. Heavy Metal whipped around a tight corner, almost as if he was trying to buck me off. I reached my arm down for the kill switch, but it was just a few inches too far away. I stretched for it, overbalancing on the fast-moving machine. My legs flung out behind me, kicking and flailing.

A final desperate extension, and I was falling. As I tumbled off, my hand swept down the stainless steel body and flicked the kill switch. I hit the floor hard and somersaulted over in time to see Heavy Metal coast to a harmless halt on his Mecanum wheels. The drone set itself down a few feet away. A final golf ball dropped out of the firing turret and rolled toward me. I picked it up. I had no idea why.

In the cowed silence that followed, the first person I saw was Brad. He raced over, scooped me up like I weighed nothing, and squeezed hard enough to collapse my rib cage. "Donnie—are you okay?"

"I *was*!" I gasped.

A loud voice cut the air. "That's *him*!" Mr. Kaminsky climbed up on a table and pointed at me. "That's the guy I saw sticking out of my truck! The same legs! The same scissor kick! He's the *real* superkid!"

Brad shook me like a rag doll. "Is that true?"

I thought of Beatrice and kept my mouth shut.

Megan stepped forward. "It *is* true. I found proof in my pool filter. Donovan's the one who saved our house."

Hundreds of pairs of eyes turned on Noah, who was just crawling out from under his chair.

Dr. Schultz's face was a thundercloud. "Noah—please explain. Did you lie to everyone?"

I watched as the terrified expression on Noah's face became suddenly peaceful, even confident.

"Of course I lied," he said reasonably. "For friend-ship."

"For *friendship*?" the superintendent echoed. "How does friendship figure into a titanic hoax perpetrated on an entire community? They named a *sandwich* after you, for crying out loud!"

"I was protecting Donovan," Noah told him righ-teously. "And he was protecting Beatrice."

"Beatrice?" the governor chimed in, irritated. "Who's Beatrice?"

"My dog, sir," Brad supplied. He turned to me. "What's Beatrice got to do with all this?"

I was determined to say nothing, but I had no con-trol over Noah's mouth.

He replied, "Donovan didn't want to get caught in Hashtag's neighborhood because Beatrice has a crimi-nal record."

The buzz of confusion that greeted that statement filled the cafeteria to the high ceilings. I knew the jig was up when I saw Hashtag and his parents pushing through the crowd toward us. There was no way to protect Brad's beloved chow chow now. I had to come clean.

"Noah was going to start a fight at the Taggarts', so I went over there to stop him," I confessed. "The thing is, I was supposed to stay away from Hashtag, because Beatrice bit him. So when all that stuff happened with the propane truck, I couldn't even admit I was on Staunton Street." Then I pulled another Donovan Classic—one that was, in a way, every bit as reckless as anything I'd ever done before. I added, "So I begged Noah to cover for me."

Okay, I didn't owe the guy any loyalty after the way he'd been treating me lately. But for all his brains, he could be like a newborn baby. How could I let him be hated by an entire town that needed someone to blame because they felt stupid for worshipping the wrong hero?

Mr. Taggart stepped forward. "Son, I can't tell you how impressed I am with your family. First, there's your brother-in-law in the armed forces. Now I find you're the real superkid, but you were willing to give up all that glory to protect a family pet. I take my hat off to you people. And I promise not to make any trouble for your dog."

The governor left, mumbling something about urgent state business. And it was as if, once he was gone, no one could remember what they'd come for in the first place. So the cafeteria emptied out quickly. The robotics team had to gather up all the golf balls and load Heavy Metal back onto the bus, but Oz said they didn't need my help. On top of everything else that had happened, we still had no idea what was wrong with our robot. One thing was sure, though: If we didn't fix it, entering any competition was out of the question.

Chloe approached me in the parking lot, looking sheepish. "I guess I was half-right, huh? Sorry, Donovan. I should have believed you."

I smiled at her. "It wasn't very believable."

"Weren't you scared?" she asked. "You know, when you were in the truck?"

I shrugged. "You know me. I never think first. If I did, I might never get out of bed."

Oz called her over to the bus, and she left me with my parents.

Mom told me how proud she was to have not just one American hero in the family but two. "And if you ever try a crazy stunt like that again," she finished, "so help me, Donnie, I'll break every bone in your body!"

So what else was new?

As we got into the station wagon, my father looked at me with a strange expression. "Superkid, huh?"

"I guess."

He shook his head. "I can't even get you to cut the grass."

## 25

# SUPERINNOCENT
## CHLOE GARFINKLE

*<< Hypothesis: It's best to get to the bottom
of a crisis right after it happens. >>*

**A**bigail pounded the keyboard at light speed, beads of perspiration standing out on her forehead. I worked almost as furiously at the computer next to hers. Across the robotics lab at the teacher's desk, Oz was hunched over his own laptop.

Our drone sat on a table at the center of the room, next to a shopping bag full of golf balls. Heavy Metal stood beside it, powered down and harmless now, but the damage had already been done—and in front of the governor and half the town, no less. That was why we were there after the rest of the robotics team had gone home. This was our best chance to find the mysterious glitch that was causing our robot to melt down.

It had been Abigail's idea to perform a diagnostic not on *all* the robot's software—that would have taken hours—but on the commands that had been executed most recently.

<< *Hypothesis: Sometimes the most obvious solutions are the hardest ones to see.* >>

"You girls should go home," Oz called wearily from across the room.

"No way," Abigail murmured without looking away from her screen.

"It wasn't your fault, Abigail," the teacher insisted. "Or yours, Chloe. Nobody can foresee every problem. System failures happen. All you can do is hope and pray that they don't happen in front of the governor." He added, a little bitterly, "Or Dr. Schultz."

If he thought that would make Abigail feel better, he'd picked the wrong kid.

"Since we have no idea what caused the malfunction,

how can we say with any confidence whose fault it was?" she demanded, her voice rising. "And even if it wasn't our fault, it might as well have been."

"If it's okay, Oz, we'd like to stay," I put in. "We're really anxious to get to the bottom of this."

The teacher nodded, then looked out the window to the parking lot. "That's Dr. Schultz's car. I have a feeling he's going to want to talk to me. Let me know if you make any progress." He headed out of the lab, his laptop under his arm.

We slogged on, energized by the knowledge that the superintendent was in the building. Neither of us put it into words, but we both understood that nothing less than the robotics program itself was at stake. The disaster had been that serious—especially to a guy like Dr. Schultz, who flipped out over anything that made the school district look bad. He went crazy over potholes in the parking lot. We could only imagine his opinion of a class project running amok in a cafeteria full of people that included the governor of the state.

I knew instantly when Abigail stumbled on something. Her bony shoulders rose up around her ears, and her fingers on the keyboard were just a blur.

"What is it?" I abandoned my own computer and wheeled my chair over beside her. "What's"—I squinted at the screen—"GradeWorm?"

"I'll tell you what it isn't," she replied grimly, scrolling through lines of code. "It isn't anything that belongs on Heavy Metal's hard drive."

I scanned the seemingly endless coded instructions that were unfurling before our eyes. Face it, I wasn't Abigail. I couldn't sight-read all this and be sure what I was looking at. But I could take a pretty good guess. "A virus?"

She shook her head. "A program. An internet bot, I think."

"Heavy Metal's not on the internet! What's a bot doing there?"

Her face was reddening to an unhealthy plum color. "What it's doing there? It's hurling golf balls at the governor, and making us look like idiots in the process!"

I just stared at her.

"Someone hid a renegade program on Heavy Metal's hard drive," she explained in a fury, "and it interfered with our software, causing all that weird behavior!"

I couldn't believe it. "But who would do something like that? Who's even capable of it?"

We looked at each other and chorused, "Noah!"

I was still confused. "Why would Noah hide a program on our robot?"

I could tell when Abigail had the answer to that question. Her face drained of all color, and her mouth formed the letter *O*. "That *maniac*!"

"What?" I almost screamed.

She scanned the lines of code, analyzing the meaning of each complicated instruction. "GradeWorm is a bot designed to hack into the school district's website so users can change their grades on the central database."

"*Noah* did that?" I was horrified. "Why? He could get A-plus-plus in everything just by showing up!"

"Who knows why?" she retorted. "It's Noah—there doesn't have to be a reason! He's a few degrees shy of a full rotation! And this time he destroyed our robot and maybe our reputations! Well, he's not going to get away with it! We have to make sure everybody knows all this is his fault and we didn't do anything wrong!"

She was 100 percent right. Noah had created an awful program nobody should ever have, and wrecked Heavy Metal in the process.

On the other hand, this was *Noah*. Okay, he was guilty, but he was also so *innocent*!

<< *Hypothesis: Some people can be guilty and innocent at the same time.* >>

Noah had just been exposed to the world as a bogus

superkid. Did we really want to pile on with all this too?

"Or," I said slowly, "we could cover for him."

She almost blew a gasket. "Oh, no you don't! That little lunatic was blessed with more brains than all the rest of us put together! Do you know how much I'd give to be inside that head of his for five minutes, just to see what it's like to be that smart? He doesn't deserve favors from us; he deserves to face the music!"

"Abigail, have a heart—"

She froze me out. "In the gifted program? Don't make me laugh!"

"Come on—"

The door was flung wide, and in scrambled Oz, his expression wild.

"What happened?" I asked.

His breath was ragged. "I went to show Dr. Schultz our operating system, and—and—" He opened his laptop on the desk in front of us. The GradeWorm software was displayed on the screen. "Wait till I get my hands on Noah Youkilis!"

I opened my mouth to speak up for Noah one more time, but no sound came out. All I could do was watch as Abigail threw him to the sharks.

She took a deep breath.

<< *Hypothesis: Calm often precedes the most violent storm.* >>

I closed my eyes.

Then she said, "Don't be hasty, Oz. There's absolutely no proof that Noah did this."

"No proof?" The teacher's eyes bulged. He scrolled down to the bottom of the page. There, beneath the final line of coding, was this message:

© by SuperkidHardcastle

# 26

# SUPERKICKED
## NOAH YOUKILIS

It was too good to last.

I don't mean my time as the superkid—although that didn't last either. I'm talking about going to regular school.

They kicked me out of Hardcastle Middle School. Expelled. Not for lying about what happened at the Mercury house and pretending to be something I wasn't. No, it was GradeWorm that did me in—the internet bot I created for the two Daniels. Dr. Schultz was unimpressed by my elegant design and next-generation coding. All he got out of it was the idea that kids could use it to change their grades to whatever they wanted them to be.

He was against it.

The really unfair part was how I got caught. Remember the safe place I thought up to hide GradeWorm after the two Daniels were too chicken to use it? I saved it on some free space on Heavy Metal's drive. It was a location where it could never interact with the robot's software.

Except it did.

Funny, I was so confident in the secure isolation of my hiding place that I never even considered the possibility that GradeWorm was the reason why the robot kept going haywire.

The world and YouTube—and, apparently, Heavy Metal's hard drive—were such complicated, interconnected, and messy systems that nothing could ever be 100 percent determinate.

It was a mistake on my part. A miscalculation.

See, this was even more proof of the amazing progress I was making at Hardcastle. Miscalculations. Mistakes. At this rate, I would be average in no time at all.

Dr. Schultz didn't agree. That was the real downside of what happened. Not only was I out of regular school, but I had to go back to the Academy. I tried to persuade Dr. Schultz what a bad idea that was. But he said the whole point of having a gifted academy was to put people like me in it.

So there I was, back in the gifted program, getting 100 percent in everything.

Yawn.

"Don't be crazy, Noah," Abigail scolded. "Hardcastle Middle might as well be a kindergarten for all they have to teach you."

"You're wrong," I told her.

Abigail didn't appreciate being wrong like I did. She scowled at me.

"Seriously," I persisted. "I *improved* there. I never improve here. There's zero opportunity for growth. I start at a hundred percent and just flatline."

"Because you're that smart," Chloe argued.

"Name one thing you improved on at Hardcastle," Donovan challenged.

"Cheerleading," I replied immediately. "I started off merely good, and now I'm fantastic. *Quod erat demonstrandum.*" The Academy stank, but at least people understood Latin here.

Luckily I didn't have to give up my cheerleading career. Just like Donovan rode the minibus to the Academy for robotics, I now rode a different minibus to Hardcastle for cheerleading. The Hornets told Coach Franco that the winning streak would be in jeopardy without me on the sidelines, and the girls all threatened to quit if I wasn't allowed to stay on the squad. Even Megan seemed to like me better now that I wasn't the superkid anymore. Maybe it was awkward to have to cheerlead side by side with your knight in shining armor. She probably had a crush on me. She definitely appreciated how I was making the squad better. She signed us all up for Marine training with Brad, and she carried the heaviest pack when we marched—with seven bricks inside it.

The girls were awesome. They never blamed me for posing as the superkid. They understood that I only did it to help out Donovan. I was worried that other people might hold it against me after the truth came out, but that didn't happen. It wasn't so much that everyone forgave me. It was more like nobody seemed to care about the whole superkid thing the way they used to. One minute, it was the biggest story in the world, and the next it just wasn't anymore.

Even Russ Trussman didn't have any hard feelings.

He called one last time after the governor's visit to confirm the facts of what had actually happened that morning on Staunton Street.

"One last thing," he said. "How did that chair get in the Mercurys' pool? I understand all the details except that one."

I frowned. I'd already explained that to him right before the governor's visit. Had he forgotten? Come to think of it, I couldn't remember him writing that part down in his notebook.

So I walked him through the details of why I'd gone to Staunton Street in the first place—to confront Hashtag about bullying Donovan. I didn't have to keep that secret anymore, since everything was out in the open now. Hashtag and I were friends, and the Taggarts had promised not to take any action against Beatrice. "No self-respecting wrestler would be caught dead without a steel chair to break over his opponent's head," I told him. "That's common knowledge."

There was a long silence on the other end of the line. I got the impression that Mr. Trussman wanted to ask another question, but he couldn't find the right words. That had always been the problem with Russ Trussman. In spite of the fact that he was a famous reporter, he wasn't very good at his job.

To nudge him along a little, I suggested that maybe he should interview Donovan, who was the *real* super-kid.

"I think Hardcastle has had enough heroes for a while," he replied wearily. "Good luck, Noah. You'll need it."

He hung up before I had a chance to inform him that I didn't need luck. I had a genius-plus IQ. I had YouTube. And I had friends—more than ever before, in fact. That was all that mattered.

Speaking of friends: Donovan and I were getting along much better. Even though we didn't go to the same school anymore, we still saw each other at robotics. And I came over to his house a lot for training and to visit Tina.

I was holding the baby on my knee—supporting her head, as recommended by the American Academy of Pediatrics—singing the formula for calculating the volume of a gas at various ocean depths, when I looked at Donovan. He was trying to get something out of Kandy's coat, which was either chewing gum or a highly advanced form of plastic explosive.

"I'm sorry," I blurted suddenly.

"For what?" He was scrubbing at the matted fur with rubbing alcohol, never glancing away from his task. "You're not the one who went dumpster-diving in the trash can." He added to Kandy, "Yeah, I'm talking about you, smart guy. Don't act so clueless."

"It's just that—" I hesitated. I wasn't good at this. Regret was kind of alien to me. But lately, I'd been haunted by an odd sense that the whole superkid episode had been hard on Donovan.

"Spit it out, Noah," he prodded.

"I'm sorry I was so good at being the superkid that I made you look bad."

He stopped working at Kandy's fur and scrutinized me for a long time. Finally, he said, "Don't worry about it."

I added generously, "You may not be a superkid, but you're a superfriend."

He laughed. "Thanks, Noah. You too."

So friendship *didn't* follow the mathematical principle of radioactive decay after all. A friendship could decay for a while and then go back to the point where it was better than ever.

# 27

# SUPERGIFTED
## DONOVAN CURTIS

"Who's my beautiful baby girl? That's right—you are. Yes!"

I pressed my ear against the wall to listen in. The words themselves weren't what surprised me. Ever since Tina was born, that kind of cooing had become a constant soundtrack in our house. No, what blew my mind was that the voice doing the cooing belonged to *Brad*!

Well, what did you know? First Lieutenant Bradley

Patterson had finally decided to throw away the Marine Corps handbook and stop speaking to his newborn daughter as if she was a cadet at Parris Island.

"I could just eat you up! Look at your cute little nosey-wosey. And your earsy-wearsy . . ."

Yikes, this was barf-worthy stuff! I'd created a monster!

" . . . and your silky-smooth fur coat!"

Fur coat?

I tiptoed out into the hall, nudged Brad's door open a crack, and peered inside.

Tina's crib was empty. The baby wasn't even in the room. Brad sat on the bed, his arms around Beatrice's bushy form, goo-gooing at his chow chow. And Beatrice seemed totally into it, sitting stock-still and gazing up at her owner with liquid eyes.

So that was how it was going to be. Brad would never follow the advice of his wing-nut, eighth-grade, civilian brother-in-law—not for humans anyway. My guidance was fit only for the dog.

And you know what? It worked. From that day forward, Beatrice forgave Brad. She abandoned me completely and followed him around everywhere, wagging and licking.

There was no explanation for it. Nothing changed.

Except for the baby talk, Brad wasn't acting much differently toward her. She still wasn't allowed to get too close to baby Tina. A door just opened, and Beatrice went through it. And because she was a dog, there was no way to ask her about it. Dogs' behavior would always remain a mystery like that.

Come to think of it, people's behavior didn't make much more sense. For instance, all of Hardcastle had idolized Noah when they believed he'd saved the Mercury house. But now that they knew it was me, nobody thought it was very important anymore. What changed? It was almost as if they'd used up all their admiration on Noah, and they didn't have any left for the real guy.

If anything, the kids at school were kind of annoyed with me. Like they'd had an idea in their heads, and I'd spoiled it. Noah had once told me that there was no contradiction in *being* the superkid without having ever saved anything. I hadn't taken it seriously at the time, but now I was starting to see his point. For sure, the reverse was true. I had done all the things that had catapulted Noah to superkid fame, and I was still about as un-super as you could get.

Kandy appreciated me, even if nobody else did. We were brothers across the species line. He was the canine version of an ungifted guy like me. Someday, I might even get him paper-trained. I wasn't holding my breath, though.

Okay, I was. But only at times like now, when I was cleaning up one of his messes. Actually, the weird part was I didn't mind all that much. Let Brad have Beatrice; Kandy would always be mine.

"Donnie—" Katie appeared in the doorway with the ever-present Tina on her shoulder.

"What's up?"

I noticed that my sister was wearing the HARD-CASTLE CHEER sweater again. Not her old one from high school. This was a gift from—of all people—Megan Mercury. Apparently, Katie used to be her cheerleading idol back in the day. Go figure.

"Brad needs you outside," she told me.

"For what?"

"Do I look like his secretary?" she asked. "Go ask him yourself."

I sighed. There was no point in putting off Brad. Tank commanders were used to being obeyed. If you didn't shake a leg, pretty soon he'd come in and shake it for you.

So I dragged myself downstairs, Kandy tripping at my heels. I stepped out the front door.

And froze.

Brad stood there, all six foot four of him, ramrod straight. He was in full dress blues, complete with white gloves and a sword tucked under his left arm. His hat was a little battered, courtesy of Kandy. But the whole effect was still pretty impressive.

He barked, "Atten-*hut*!"

That was when I saw the others. The cheerleaders, in uniform, were lined up like an honor guard—including Noah, who was at attention, and not praying-mantis-like at all. Off to the side, the Daniels were leaning on each other and grinning at me.

"What's this about?" I asked Brad.

"Donovan James Curtis!" Brad boomed. "For conspicuous bravery diverting a propane tanker from colliding with a home, showing no regard for your own life and safety . . ." He reached into a velvet box and took out a round silver medal on a pale blue ribbon.

I gawked. "Whose medal is that?"

"It's yours, dummy," Katie called from the front porch. "It's the one Governor Holland brought to give to Noah. Brad drove to the state house and explained how it should have gone to you."

Brad went on, "I hereby act as Governor Holland's

proxy as I present you with the State Youth Award for Valor and Community Service. Congratulations."

Kind of embarrassed, I bowed my head as he placed the ribbon around my neck. It itched through my T-shirt. In the background, I could hear the Daniels snickering.

"I'm not really the medals type," I mumbled to Brad.

"Well, get used to it. You deserve this, Donnie. Most guys would have stood there and watched that truck hit that house and explode. Maybe me, for one. I don't know if that makes you a superkid, but you'll always be super in my book."

Funny—I never cared much about Brad's opinion of me before. But when a real hero thought you were a hero too, that meant a lot. I didn't realize how much.

For a guy who wasn't gifted *or* super, I felt pretty supergifted just then.

# 28

## JUST PLAIN SUPER
### NOAH YOUKILIS

I found the envelope in a stack of old mail on the kitchen counter. It was addressed: *To the Parents of Noah Youkilis* and the letterhead was from Hardcastle Middle School. At first I thought it must have been the official notification that I was kicked out. But then I saw it was postmarked two days *before* the governor's visit.

I slid the letter out and read it.

*Dear Mr. and Mrs. Youkilis,*
*This is to inform you that, due to disappointing*
*academic performance in his current placement, your son*
*Noah has been recommended for remedial classes . . .*

The letter blurred as my eyes filled with tears. The joy and wonder that surged into my heart were like nothing I'd ever experienced before, not even when I watched my first YouTube video.

Remedial classes! Oh, sure, it had come too late. But that didn't change the fact that I'd done it!

If I could qualify for remedial classes with a 206 IQ, then I was a new and truly original kind of superkid!

No gifted program could hold me down. For Noah Youkilis, the sky was the limit.

Turn the page for a sneak peek
at Gordon Korman's

# THE UNTEACHABLES

# One

## Kiana Roubini

It's no fun riding to school with Stepmonster—not with Chauncey screaming his lungs out in the back seat.

Don't get me wrong. I'd cry too if I'd just figured out that Stepmonster is my mother. But at seven months old, I don't think he's processed that yet. He just cries. He cries when he's hungry; he cries when he's full; he cries when he's tired; he cries when he wakes up after a long nap. Basically, any day that ends in a *y*, Chauncey cries.

There also seems to be a connection between his volume control and the gas pedal of the SUV. The louder he howls, the faster Stepmonster drives.

"Who's a happy baby?" she coos over her shoulder into the back seat, where the rear-facing car seat is anchored. "Who's a happy big boy?"

"Not Chauncey, that's for sure," I tell her. "Hey—school zone. You better slow down."

She speeds up. "Motion is soothing to a baby."

Maybe so. But as we slalom up the driveway, swerving around parked parents dropping off their kids, and screech to a halt by the entrance, it turns out to be one motion too many. Chauncey throws up his breakfast. Suddenly, there's cereal on the ceiling and dripping down the windows. That's another thing about Chauncey. His stomach is a food expander. It goes in a teaspoon and comes out five gallons.

"Get out of the car!" Stepmonster orders frantically.

"You have to come in with me," I protest. "They won't let me register without an adult."

She looks frazzled, and I guess I don't blame her. That much baby puke must be hard to face. "I'll run home, change him, and wipe down the car. Wait for me. Ten minutes—fifteen at the most."

What can I do? I haul my backpack out of the SUV, and she zooms off around the circular drive. I don't even have the chance to make my usual Parmesan cheese joke—that's what it smells like when Chauncey barfs. When I first came from California to stay with Dad and Stepmonster, I thought they ate a lot of Italian food. That was a disappointment—one of many.

So there I am in front of Greenwich Middle School, watching swarms of kids arriving for the first day of classes. A few of them glance in my direction, but not many. New girl; who cares? Actually, the new girl doesn't much care either. I'm a short-timer—I'm only in Greenwich for a couple of months while Mom is off in Utah shooting a movie. She's not a star or anything like that, but this could be her big break. After years of paying the bills with bit parts in sitcoms and TV commercials, she finally landed an independent film. Well, no way could I go with her for eight weeks— not that I was invited.

Eventually, a bell rings and the crowd melts into the school. No Stepmonster. I'm officially late, which isn't the best way to start my career in Greenwich. But short-timers don't stress over things like that.

Long before it could come back to haunt me on a report card, I'll be ancient history.

I check on my phone. It's been twenty minutes since "ten minutes—fifteen at the most." That's SST—Stepmonster Standard Time. I try calling, but she doesn't pick up. Maybe that means she's on her way and will be here any second.

But a lot of seconds tick by. No barf-encrusted SUV.

With a sigh, I sit myself down on the bench at student drop-off and prop my backpack up on the armrest beside me. Stepmonster—her real name is Louise—isn't all that monstrous when you think about it. She's way less out of touch than Dad, which might be because she's closer to my age than his. She isn't exactly thrilled with the idea of having an eighth grader dropped in her lap right when she's getting the hang of being a new mom. She's trying to be nice to me—she just isn't succeeding. Like when she strands me in front of a strange school when she's supposed to be here to get me registered.

The roar of an engine jolts me back to myself. For a second I think it must be her. But no—a rusty old pickup truck comes sailing up the roadway, going much faster than even Stepmonster would dare. As it reaches the bend in the circular drive, the front tire climbs the curb, and the pickup is coming right at me. Acting on instinct alone, I hurl myself over the back of the bench and out of the way.

The truck misses the bench by about a centimeter. The side mirror knocks my book bag off the armrest, sending it airborne. The contents—binders, papers, pencil case, gym shorts, sneakers, lunch—are scattered to the four winds, raining down on the pavement.

The pickup screeches to a halt. The driver jumps out and starts rushing after my fluttering stuff. As he runs, papers fly out of his shirt pocket, and he's chasing his own things, not just mine.

I join the hunt, and that's when I get my first look at the guy. He's a kid—like, around my age! "Why are you driving?" I gasp, still in shock from the near miss.

"I have a license," he replies, like it's the most normal thing in the world.

"No way!" I shoot back. "You're no older than I am!"

"I'm fourteen." He digs around in his front pocket and pulls out a laminated card. It's got a picture of his stupid face over the name Parker Elias. At the top it says: PROVISIONAL LICENSE.

"Provisional?" I ask.

"I'm allowed to drive for the family business," he explains.

"Which is what—a funeral parlor? You almost killed me."

"Our farm," he replies. "I take produce to the market. Plus, I take my grams to the senior center. She's super old and doesn't drive anymore."

I've never met a farmer before. There aren't a lot of them in LA. I knew Greenwich was kind of the boonies, but I never expected to be going to school with Old MacDonald.

He hands me my book bag with my stuff crammed in every which way. There's a gaping hole where the mirror blasted through the vinyl.

"I'm running late," he stammers. "Sorry about the backpack." He jumps in the pickup, wheels it into a parking space, and races into the building, studiously avoiding my glare.

Still no sign of Stepmonster on the horizon. I call again. Straight to voice mail.

I decide to tackle the school on my own. Maybe I can get a head start filling out forms or something.

The office is a madhouse. It's packed with kids who a) lost their schedules, b) don't understand their schedules, or c) are trying to get their schedules changed. When I tell the harassed secretary that I'm waiting for my parent and/or guardian so I can register, she just points to a chair and ignores me.

Even though I have nothing against Greenwich Middle School, I decide to hate it. Who can blame me? It's mostly Chauncey's fault, but let's not forget Parker McFarmer and his provisional license.

My phone pings. A text from Stepmonster: *Taking Chauncey to pediatrician. Do your best without me. Will get there ASAP.*

The secretary comes out from behind the counter and stands before me, frowning. "We don't use our phones in school. You'll have to turn that off and leave it in your locker."

"I don't have a locker," I tell her. "I just moved here. I have no idea where I'm supposed to be."

She plucks a paper from the sheaf sticking out of the hole in my backpack. "It's right here on your schedule."

"Schedule?" Where would I get a schedule? I don't even officially go to school here yet.

"You're supposed to be in room 117." She rattles off a complicated series of directions. "Now, off you go."

And off I go. I'm so frazzled that I'm halfway down the main hall before I glance at the paper that's supposed to be a schedule. It's a schedule, all right—just not mine.

7

At the top, it says: ELIAS, PARKER. GRADE: 8.

This is Parker McFarmer's schedule! It must have gotten mixed up with my papers when we were gathering up all my stuff.

I take three steps back in the direction of the office and freeze. I don't want to face that secretary again. There's no way she's going to register me without Stepmonster. And if there's a backlog at the pediatrician's, I'm going to be sitting in that dumb chair all day. No, thanks.

I weigh my options. It's only a fifteen-minute walk home. But home isn't really home, and I don't want to be there any more than I want to be here. If I went to all the trouble of waking up and getting ready for school, then school is where I might as well be.

My eyes return to Parker's schedule. Room 117. Okay, it's not *my* class, but it's *a* class. And really, who cares? It's not like I'm going to learn anything in the next two months—at least nothing I can't pick up when I get back to civilization. I'm a pretty good student. And when Stepmonster finally gets here, they can page me and send me to the right place—not that I'll learn anything there either. I've already learned the one lesson Greenwich Middle School has to teach me: fourteen-year-olds shouldn't drive.

That's when I learn lesson number two: this place is a maze. My school in LA is all outdoors—you step out of class and you're in glorious sunshine. You know where you're going next because you can see it across the quad. And the numbers make sense. Here, 109 is next to 111, but the room next to that is labeled STORAGE CLOSET E61-B2. Go figure.

I ask a couple of kids, who actually try to tell me that there's no such room as 117.

"There has to be," I tell the second guy. "I'm in it." I show him the schedule, careful to cover the name with my thumb.

"Wait." His brow furrows. "What's"—he points to the class description—"SCS-8?"

I blink. Instead of a normal schedule, where you go to a different class every period, this says Parker stays in room 117 all day. Not only that, but under SUB-JECT, it repeats the code SCS-8 for every hour except LUNCH at 12:08.

"Oh, here it is." I skip to the bottom, where there's a key explaining what the codes mean. "SCS-8—Self-Contained Special Eighth-Grade Class."

He stares at me. "The *Unteachables*?"

"Unteachables?" I echo.

He reddens. "You know, like the Untouchables.

Only—uh"—babbling now—"these kids aren't un-touchable. They're—well—unteachable. Bye!" He rushes off down the hall.

And I just know. I could read it in his face, but I didn't even need that much information. Where would you stick a guy who could annihilate a back-pack with a half-ton pickup truck? The Unteachables are the dummy class. We have a couple of groups like that in my middle school in California too. We call them the Disoriented Express, but it's the same thing. Probably every school has that.

I almost march back to the office to complain when I remember I've got nothing to complain about. Nobody put *me* in the Unteachables—just Parker. From what I've seen, he's in the right place.

I picture myself, sitting in the office all day, waiting for Stepmonster to arrive. *If* she arrives. Chauncey's health scares—which happen roughly every eight minutes—stress her out to the point where she can't focus on anything else. To quote Dad, "Jeez, Louise." He really says that—an example of the sense of humor of the non-California branch of my family.

So I go to room 117—turns out, it's in the far corner of the school, over by the metal shop, the home and careers room, and the custodian's office. You have to walk past the gym, and the whole hallway smells like old sweat socks mixed with a faint barbecue scent. It's only temporary, I remind myself. And since my whole time in Greenwich is temporary anyway, it's more like temporary squared.

Besides—dummy class, Disoriented Express, Unteachables—so what? Okay, maybe they're not academic superstars, but they're just kids, no different from anybody else. Even Parker—he's a menace to society behind the wheel of that truck, but besides that he's a normal eighth grader, like the rest of us.

Seriously, how unteachable can these Unteachables be?

I push open the door and walk into room 117.

A plume of smoke is pouring out the single open window. It's coming from the fire roaring in the wastebasket in the center of the room. A handful of kids are gathered around it, toasting marshmallows skewered on the end of number two pencils. Parker is one of them, his own marshmallow blackened like a charcoal briquette.

An annoyed voice barks, "Hey, shut the door! You want to set off the smoke detector in the hall?"

Oh my God, I'm with the Unteachables.

# More favorites by
# GORDON KORMAN

## THE MASTERMINDS SERIES

BALZER + BRAY

*An Imprint of HarperCollinsPublishers*